BARRY WYNN

LECTOR HOUSE PUBLIC DOMAIN WORKS

This book is a result of an effort made by Lector House towards making a contribution to the preservation and repair of original classic literature. The original text is in the public domain in the United States of America, and possibly other countries depending upon their specific copyright laws.

In an attempt to preserve, improve and recreate the original content, certain conventional norms with regard to typographical mistakes, hyphenations, punctuations and/or other related subject matters, have been corrected upon our consideration. However, few such imperfections might not have been rectified as they were inherited and preserved from the original content to maintain the authenticity and construct, relevant to the work. The work might contain a few prior copyright references as well as page references which have been retained, wherever considered relevant to the part of the construct. We believe that this work holds historical, cultural and/or intellectual importance in the literary works community, therefore despite the oddities, we accounted the work for print as a part of our continuing effort towards preservation of literary work and our contribution towards the development of the society as a whole, driven by our beliefs.

We are grateful to our readers for putting their faith in us and accepting our imperfections with regard to preservation of the historical content. We shall strive hard to meet up to the expectations to improve further to provide an enriching reading experience.

Though, we conduct extensive research in ascertaining the status of copyright before redeveloping a version of the content, in rare cases, a classic work might be incorrectly marked as not-in-copyright. In such cases, if you are the copyright holder, then kindly contact us or write to us, and we shall get back to you with an immediate course of action.

HAPPY READING!

BARRY WYNN

GEORGE BARTON

ISBN: 978-93-90294-46-6

Published: -

© 2020
LECTOR HOUSE LLP

LECTOR HOUSE LLP
E-MAIL: lectorpublishing@gmail.com

BARRY STOOD FOR A MOMENT UNDECIDED WHICH WAY TO TURN

BARRY WYNN
OR
THE ADVENTURES OF A PAGE BOY IN THE UNITED STATES CONGRESS

BY

GEORGE BARTON

AUTHOR OF "THE MYSTERY OF CLEVERLY," "ADVENTURES OF THE WORLD'S GREATEST DETECTIVES," ETC.

ILLUSTRATED BY
JOHN HUYBERS

TO
HERBERT AND GEORGE

CONTENTS

Chapter	Page
I. UNDER THE BIG DOME	1
II. THE NAVAL REPAIR STATION	5
III. THE NEW PAGE	11
IV. VISIONS OF GREATNESS	17
V. A WINK AND A NOD	21
VI. HUDSON STRIKES A SNAG	26
VII. BARRY STUMBLES	32
VIII. AN UNEXPECTED MOVE	37
IX. ON THE TRAIL OF JOE HART	41
X. SUSPENSE	48
XI. DISCORD AND DEFEAT	52
XII. SMITHERS TO THE RESCUE	58
XIII. A LITTLE PILGRIMAGE	63
XIV. BARRY FALLS A SECOND TIME	69
XV. BARRY REDEEMS HIMSELF	75
XVI. A CALL OF THE HOUSE	80
XVII. THE MISSING BILL	86
XVIII. RUMORS OF WAR	90
XIX. SORELY TEMPTED	94
XX. HUDSON PLAYS POLITICS	100

CONTENTS

XXI.	CONWAY MAKES A HIT	105
XXII.	PROOF CONCLUSIVE	108
XXIII.	WHAT BARRY OVERHEARD	112
XXIV.	THE LAST STAND	117
XXV.	A RACE AGAINST TIME	122
XXVI.	THE HOME COMING	129

LIST OF ILLUSTRATIONS

Page

I. Barry stood for a moment undecided which way to turn v

II. "I want you to make a solemn promise to me" 47

III. His eyes were never removed from the boy's face for a moment 98

IV. The young page boy was enjoying it to the fullest 125

BARRY WYNN

CHAPTER I

UNDER THE BIG DOME

Barry Wynn grabbed the rail of the day coach of the Washington Express and swung himself on to the platform of the car with the ease and enthusiasm of a healthy boy of fifteen. The world had suddenly expanded for him and he was aglow with life and vitality. He had been appointed a page in the National House of Representatives, and now, in response to a telegram from Congressman Carlton, he was about to go to the Capitol to take the oath of office and assume the duties of his position.

His heart was swelling with the thought of the big things in the future. He had studied the history of his country in the Cleverly schools and he had also an intelligent idea of the great organization which we call the United States Government. He had not neglected to read the debates of Congress in the daily newspapers and now he was to be in the midst of great events, to be a part of our great central law-making machine at Washington. He was dwelling on this thought when his attention was attracted by a voice from the crowd on the platform.

"Barry! Barry!" it shouted above the puffing of the locomotive, "Wait a minute."

The call came from Mr. Smithers who had been his school teacher and who now was also the President of the local Board of Trade. Barry leaned over the platform and Mr. Smithers, making his way through the throng, handed the boy a bulky manilla envelope fastened with rubber bands.

"Give this to Congressman Carlton as soon as you arrive in Washington," he said.

"All right," replied Barry.

"Be careful with it," continued the man; "it contains a matter of vital importance to the people of Cleverly."

"You can depend on me," was the confident response.

The conductor gave the final warning, the bell began to clang, and the train steamed out of the station with Barry standing on the platform waving good-bye to his faithful friends. His eyes were so dimmed with tears that could not be suppressed that he scarcely recognized the upturned faces that were shedding their good will upon him in such generous measure. One exception to this was his mother. She seemed to stand out from the crowd, fluttering a little lace handkerchief until the station at Cleverly became a mere speck in the distance.

The journey in itself was uneventful, although it furnished constant interest and amusement for the boy who was about to get his first large view of the world. Thoughtful ones at home had provided him with a dainty box of lunch, and before long he was attacked with the pangs of hunger and devoured every last scrap of the cake and fruit and sandwiches.

Finally, after a ride of nine or ten hours the city of Washington began to come in view. The outlying section was not very inviting, but as the train came near to its destination the view improved. A sudden turning of the train brought the magnificent dome of the Capitol into the range of his vision. Barry gasped with wonder and delight. It was as though some magician had waved his wand over vacant space and suddenly brought the wonderful creation into being. In all of the time he was in Washington Barry never lost his sense of delight at each recurring sight of that noble specimen of architecture. To him the solidity and beauty of the Capitol seemed symbolic of the strength and splendor of the Republic.

As the train came nearer and nearer to the new Union Station the boy was enabled to get a closer view of the great structure which stood outlined on the horizon in all of its majestic proportions. He had an instinctive sense of the beautiful and the symmetrical pile of marble filled him with an unexplainable joy. The main building, with its two finely designed wings, more than realized Barry's anticipations. But it was the dome rather than the Capitol itself, which kept him under its magic spell. He felt for the first time the full force of the poet's words, that "a thing of beauty is a joy forever." The vaulted roof of the rotunda, with its gradual swelling sprang into the air so gracefully that one could hardly look upon it as a thing of iron and steel and marble. And overtopping it all was the colossal statue of Freedom, typifying everything for which the Republic was founded and maintained.

The cry of "All out for Washington" brought to an end Barry's meditations, and also announced the fact that he had finally reached his destination. He picked up his suitcase and hastened out of the train and into the great Union Station which burst upon his astonished vision like another scene from the Arabian Nights. It was so great and so impressive that it fairly took his breath away. In a few minutes he was seated in a trolley car and on his way toward the Capitol. He was so eager to see everything that was to be seen on the way that he almost twisted his neck out of shape. In a very short time the car reached the foot of the hill where the great edifice is located. When Barry alighted he stood for a moment undecided which way to turn. There seemed to be all sorts of entrances to the building. He chose the nearest one, which led him to the basement of the great structure. Looking about, he saw an elevator standing with the door invitingly open. Without further ado, he hustled into the door. The attendant turned to him with a smile:

"Have you got your credentials?" he asked, tauntingly.

"My credentials," retorted Barry; "what do you mean?"

"I simply want to know whether you are a member of the Supreme Court."

"Why?"

"Because this elevator is for the exclusive use of members of the Supreme Court."

And so it proved to be. Barry turned aside a little bit confused at his first lesson in American democracy. Finally he found an elevator that was used by the public. He boarded it and in a few minutes found himself standing in the centre of the rotunda of the Capitol. It is, as most boys are aware, the great hall which stands in the centre of the Capitol between the House of Representatives and the United States Senate.

Barry set his suitcase on the floor and gazed up at the interior of the vast dome, spellbound with wonder and delight. The light, coming through the windows of the great ceiling, revealed a wilderness of art. In the very centre he beheld the marvelous allegorical fresco called the "Apotheosis of Washington." Beneath this were designs in panels and medallions showing Raleigh, Columbus, Cabot, La Salle, and the other great characters that Barry had studied about in school, and below these he gazed on a series of brilliant pictures showing scenes in the Revolutionary war.

How long he remained there in this attitude of wrapt admiration he could not tell, but when he glanced down at the floor to look for his suitcase, he found that it was gone. He rushed over to a gray-coated guide:

"Did you see anything of my suitcase?" he cried in alarm.

"Your suitcase," smiled the man; "I didn't know you had one."

"I had a minute ago," said Barry; "I set it on the floor here and now it is gone."

"Where could it go to if you had it by your side?"

"Why, I was looking at the pictures in the ceiling," said the agitated boy, "and someone must have crept along and stolen it."

"Well, I didn't see anything of it," was the calm response.

In despair, Barry ran from one person to another until the marble space below the dome was a scene of unusual excitement. In the midst of the agitation a bright-looking, well-dressed young man came striding across the hallway leading from the House of Representatives. He noticed the stir, and something about Barry's manner attracted him. He went up to the boy and said in kindly tones:

"What's the trouble, my son?"

Barry explained as best he could.

"Do you expect to meet someone here?" asked the stranger.

"I do. I was to report to Congressman Carlton."

"Why, I know him well," was the comment of the young man. "He is one of my best friends. We will have to see if we can't recover your suitcase for you."

At that moment the alert young man happened to see a red-headed youngster peeping from behind one of the pillars that supported the dome. Instantly he understood the situation.

"Joe," he called, in authoritative tones, "come here at once."

Joe, thus called, responded obediently. The stranger took Barry by the arm, and pointing to the other, said:

"This is Mr. Joseph Hart, one of the pages of the House of Representatives. Joseph, I want you to meet Mr. Barry Wynn, who is to become your associate."

"Hello," said Joe.

"How are you?" greeted Barry, taking the outstretched hand.

"Joe," continued the gentleman, "get the young man his property."

Very sheepishly Joe went behind the pillar and, bringing out the suitcase, handed it to Barry.

"Now, I will introduce myself," said the stranger, with an engaging smile. "My name is Felix Conway. I am the correspondent of a New York newspaper, and if you ever need any assistance while you are in Washington, don't fail to call on me."

"Thank you," was the grateful reply, "I am not likely to forget you."

"Now, Joe," said the correspondent, turning to the second boy again, "why did you take Mr. Wynn's suitcase?"

Joe gazed at the floor in an embarrassed manner for a moment and then, raising his head, said defiantly:

"I couldn't help it. He looked so green that I simply couldn't resist hiding his bag."

"Well," said Mr. Conway, "if you hope to be respected in this world, you'll have to resist a good many temptations."

At this point in the conversation, Congressman Carlton, of all persons in the world, came along. He recognized Barry at once, and going over, shook his hand warmly. He also talked pleasantly with Mr. Conway concerning matters in which they were both interested.

"Barry," he said, finally, "I'm awfully busy this afternoon, but I'm going to put you in care of Joe Hart here. He'll take you to a pleasant boarding-house and see that you are properly installed. Report to me here in the Capitol at ten o'clock in the morning. In the meantime, Joe will post you on your duties. You will find him a very nice boy."

"Yes," said Barry, gazing at Joe somewhat skeptically, "I suppose I will find him to be a very nice boy."

CHAPTER II
THE NAVAL REPAIR STATION

Mr. Carlton had only gone a few yards when Barry suddenly remembered the bulky manilla envelope that had been entrusted to his care as the train was leaving Cleverly. He ran after the Congressman and handed him the package. Mr. Carlton opened it in the boy's presence and his eyes lighted with pleasure.

"It's just what I've been waiting for, Conway," he said to his newspaper friend.

"Good; then you can present the whole business to the Secretary today."

"Precisely; that's what I intend to do."

"Suppose you take Barry along with you," suggested the correspondent.

"A good idea. I might want to send for some papers."

"Would he know where to go?" asked Conway, laughingly. "You know he's a stranger in a strange land."

"That's easily fixed," smiled the Congressman.

"How?"

"We'll take Joe along as a guide for Barry."

The two men and boys boarded a Pennsylvania Avenue trolley and were soon proceeding to the other end of the thoroughfare.

"My boy," said Mr. Carlton to Barry, "I think we might as well take you into our confidence."

"Yes, sir."

"Years ago, when your father and I were young men we conceived the idea that the Government should build a great naval supply station at Cleverly. He even went so far as to draw up rough plans. But the time was not ripe for it and the notion was abandoned. Since your good father's death there have been spasmodic attempts to revive the plan, but they never amounted to anything. Now, however, the conditions are all favorable, and I believe that with a little strategy and a great deal of industry, I can win the fight and make Cleverly a household name in the United States instead of a mere speck on the map."

"That would be splendid," cried Barry, his eyes glowing with pleasure.

"The big secret," continued the Congressman, "is the fact that the Government is now ready to act."

"Do you mean that they're going to build a station at Cleverly?" asked Barry, excitedly.

Mr. Carlton laughed.

"No; hardly that. I mean that the officials of the Government who have charge of our Navy have decided that we need a new Naval Repair Station. It remains for Congress to say where the station shall be located and to appropriate the money to pay for it. Now, I think, and Mr. Conway thinks, too, that the City of Cleverly can furnish the ideal site for this station."

"I don't suppose," chimed in the journalist, "that Barry can have much interest in the subject."

"Yes, I have," exclaimed the boy; "I think it's real exciting."

Both men laughed at the boy's enthusiasm.

"The excitement," observed the journalist, "will come when it becomes known that the Government intends to build the new station."

"When will it become known?"

"Very soon, I think. Mr. Carlton is going to have an interview with the Secretary of the Navy this afternoon. A great deal depends on the result of that talk."

Little Joe Hart had been listening to the conversation with great intentness. He looked up now with a comical twist of the mouth.

"Mr. Conway," he exclaimed, with mock seriousness, "you can depend on my support."

They all laughed heartily at this sally. Mr. Carlton turned to the newspaper man:

"You see," he said, "we have two young gentlemen with us already."

"Yes," was the retort, "but, unfortunately, they have no votes."

"They will have some day," commented the Congressman soberly, "and I hope they will exercise that power for the good of the country."

By this time the car had reached the Treasury Department and was going around the massive pile of granite which houses the officials and the employees who look after the finances of the nation. Mr. Carlton and his friends alighted at the next corner and walked the remainder of the distance to their destination. They passed the White House, the modest looking dwelling which is the home of the President of the United States. Barry looked at it curiously.

"What do you think of it?" asked Mr. Conway.

Barry hesitated.

"Come out with it," insisted the journalist.

"Well," said the boy reluctantly, "it doesn't look much."

Mr. Conway laughed.

"That's the opinion of most strangers. But as you grow older you will realize that it typifies the strength and simplicity of the people. We have wealth enough to give the President a palace that would rival the homes of the sovereigns of Europe, but, thank goodness, we haven't the desire."

The large stone building, which is the headquarters of the State, War and Navy Departments, was now in sight. As they walked up the high steps of the main entrance, Barry and the journalist found themselves temporarily separated from Mr. Carlton and Joe Hart. It gave Mr. Conway an opportunity of speaking of the Congressman.

"He's one of nature's noblemen," he said, fervently. "I've been here many years," he added, "and I've seen public men come and go, but I never met a cleaner, abler man than John Carlton. Only his modesty has prevented him from being the leader of Congress. He's as clean as a hound's tooth, but he would no more boast of his integrity, than he would brag of saying his prayers. He takes it as a matter of course. He despises grafters, but he also detests self-sufficient reformers who are forever flaunting their virtues in the face of the public. But," with a laugh, "I'm afraid I'm talking over your head, Barry."

"Not at all," retorted the boy. "I know just what you mean; and, besides, I love to hear anyone talk about Mr. Carlton. He was my father's best friend. That's why he had me appointed a page boy. He says it will give me a chance to see life and mix with big people and that it may lead to something better."

"That's true, and I think that even in your modest position you may be very useful to him."

"I hope so. He seems very much interested in the Naval Repair Station."

"It's the biggest thing he has ever attempted. If he succeeds the people of Cleverly will never forget him. It will mean that he will not have to fight for re-election at the end of every two years. In short it will be a monument to him."

At the head of the steps the two were joined by Mr. Carlton and Joe Hart. They proceeded along the corridor and then up another flight of stairs and presently were ushered into the office of the Secretary of the Navy. The two boys seated themselves on a leather covered sofa near the door, while the Congressman and Mr. Conway walked up to a desk where a young man was writing. He greeted them pleasantly, took their cards and disappeared into a smaller apartment in the rear of the large room. He returned in a few moments followed by an older man. The newcomer hurried over to where the Congressman was standing.

"Hello, Carlton," he cried, cheerily, "I'm glad to see you."

"The pleasure is mutual, Mr. Secretary," smiled the statesman.

"And you too, Conway," exclaimed the cabinet officer, extending his hand to the newspaper man.

The three of them took chairs. The Secretary looked at his visitors inquiringly.

"What's in the wind?" he asked, in his affable way. "It must be important when a Congressman and a journalist call together."

"It is," said Mr. Carlton, soberly. "It's about the proposed new Naval Repair Station."

"So that's got out, has it?" he remarked, musingly.

"Well, it's not exactly public property, but we've learned enough to know that Congress will take up the matter at this session."

"Really, it's no secret," admitted the Secretary, "and I'm frank enough to say that we need it very badly at this time. What's the use of spending millions of dollars in creating a first-class Navy unless we keep the battleships in first-class condition. We have a number of good navy yards, but we could use an additional Naval Repair Station to great advantage."

"I know that, and I'm going to offer a bill in Congress at an early day."

"You are?"

"I am, and I would naturally like to have the support of the Department."

"Of course," said the Secretary, hesitatingly, "it would be impossible to pledge myself in advance."

"I understand that perfectly," was the prompt reply. "I have been on the Naval Committee of the House long enough to know that these things must come up in an orderly manner and go through the regular channels."

"Certainly, certainly," echoed the cabinet officer, relieved to know that he was not going to be asked to depart from the usual method of procedure.

"I came today," continued the Congressman, "to show you a set of plans that have been prepared for a Naval Repair Station at Cleverly. I don't want to go at this matter blindly. I want you to look at our papers. Of course, later on they will be submitted to any Board of Experts that you may see fit to appoint."

"I'm sure that I would be delighted to look them over," was the quick response.

Thereupon Mr. Carlton drew forth the bulky envelope that had been entrusted to Barry on his departure from Cleverly. The Secretary became interested at once. In order to get a better view of the papers the three men walked over to a large flat-top table in the centre of the room. Here the blue prints were spread out and held down with paperweights in order that they might be intelligently studied. The Congressman, who knew his subject by heart, explained the advantages to be gained by locating the station at Cleverly. The Secretary asked many questions, which were answered promptly, satisfactorily and with confidence.

"How much of an appropriation did you think of asking for?"

"A million dollars," replied the Congressman.

"That would not pay the entire cost of the station," said the Secretary.

"No; but it would answer all present needs. Additions could be made from time to time."

Presently the Secretary pressed a button and a messenger appeared.

"Tell the Admiral I would like to see him at his convenience," he said.

In a few minutes an old gentleman, with snow white hair and moustache and ruddy cheeks, entered. He was faultlessly, almost nattily, dressed and he had an alertness about him which suggested that he might have discovered the fountain of eternal youth, whose source had been so vainly sought by the gallant Ponce de Leon.

"That's the Admiral," whispered Joe to Barry from his secluded corner of the leather sofa.

"What? The real Admiral?"

"Sure."

"Where's his cocked hat and his sword and his uniform?"

"Oh, say," cried Joe, disgusted at such evident lack of knowledge, "he doesn't wear them in his office."

"Where does he wear them?"

"When he's fighting—on the quarter deck of his flagship."

"He doesn't look like a fighter."

This was too much for Mr. Joseph Hart. He stuffed his handkerchief in his mouth to keep from screaming. He butted his head against the cushioned back of the sofa, and he performed various other silent, but none the less effective, gymnastic exercises. After he had exhausted his merriment, he turned to the Cleverly boy and said, reproachfully:

"Can he fight? Why that man sunk the entire navy of a great European nation in about twenty minutes."

"Twenty minutes?" gasped Barry, awe stricken.

"It was less than that," cried Joe, following up his advantage, "it happened this way. The Admiral was taking breakfast in the cabin of his vessel with some friends. He took a sip of his coffee and then said, 'please excuse me.' He went up on deck, and in a few minutes he returned to finish his coffee, saying, 'ha, I'm glad that's done.'"

"What had he done?" asked Barry.

"Sunk the Spanish navy."

"He doesn't act like a ferocious man."

"Real fighters never do," said Joe.

In the meantime the newcomer had joined the Secretary of the Navy and had been presented to the Congressman and the journalist. He was asked to examine the plans. He did so, at first in a perfunctory manner. But presently he became interested, and went over the blue prints with greater care. Finally he began to ask questions.

"Where would you put the dry dock?" he queried.

"Right there," replied the Congressman, indicating the spot with the tip of his little finger.

"This looks as if it might be a fresh water basin," suggested the Admiral.

"It is."

"And yet you are near the ocean."

"Within two miles of it."

Presently the Admiral finished his inspection of the plans. He leaned back in his chair, with his eyes half closed. The other three men looked at him intently. His expert opinion was of the highest value.

"Well," said the Secretary, finally, "what do you think of it?"

"Splendid," was the reply. "It looks as if it had been carved by nature for our present needs."

Five minutes later the Congressman was on his way back to the Capitol. He was bubbling over with good humor. He put his hand on Barry Wynn's shoulder:

"We've got a bully start, Barry," he said. "I do believe you're going to be my mascot."

CHAPTER III
THE NEW PAGE

After a few minutes at the Capitol with Congressman Carlton, Barry found himself walking along the streets of Washington with Master Joe Hart, who had graciously volunteered to pilot him to his boarding house, which was located on a street radiating from one of the avenues surrounding the Treasury Department. It was some distance from the hall of the House of Representatives, but as Barry desired to see as much of the city as possible, they walked instead of taking a trolley car.

The two boys made the trip by way of Pennsylvania Avenue, and at every turn in that noble thoroughfare, Barry found himself gasping with undisguised admiration. Joe Hart, who had lived in Washington for a number of years, and who was old in the ways of the world, seemed greatly amused at the frank astonishment of his companion; in fact, Master Joe indulged in a good deal of sarcasm. He told Barry that if he did not stop looking up at the buildings, he would get a kink in the neck and that would disbar him from the position as page in Congress. He wanted to know how crops were coming on "down home"; whether they were having much rain in Cleverly, and finally asked him if this year's corn would be equal to the kind that was grown last year. Barry took all of this with perfect good nature. He realized that Joe was worldly-wise, and that his manners were not as good as they might be, but something about the Washington boy attracted him mightily.

Finally they reached the boarding house. It was a three-story brick house with an air of genteel decay about it. Joe, who had a latch key, walked in without knocking. As they passed the parlor an elderly lady, who stood at the window, approached them.

"Mrs. Johnson," said Hart, "this is Barry Wynn, who is to live here for a little while."

The lady approached Barry with a smile and shook hands with him cordially.

"Mr. Carlton has been telling me about you," she said graciously, "and I think I can give you a third story back room that will suit your purposes."

"Thank you," said Barry.

"If you will come this way I will show you the room."

The boarding house mistress and the two boys walked to the third story and looked at the room that had been assigned to Barry. It was plainly but neatly furnished. The outlook was very pleasant, because for a distance of many blocks there were no buildings to obstruct the view, and most of the surrounding plots were tastefully laid out in grass and flowers. Barry learned later that the cause of this unusually luxurious outlook was a public park which was almost on the edge of Mrs. Johnson's dwelling.

"I can give you this room, with board," said Mrs. Johnson, interrupting the boy's musings, "for six dollars a week."

It seemed like a large sum to Barry, but he said bravely, and with a show of cheerfulness: "All right, Mrs. Johnson; I'll take it."

Supper at the Johnson boarding house was a very modest meal, and after it was over Barry and Joe went out, in order that the new boy might have some idea of the national capital in the evening. Barry found that the city was well paved and well lighted. It was all very interesting, but he had traveled a great distance that day and the excitement of the occasion served to add to the fatigue, so that when he heard a neighboring clock strike ten, he intimated a desire to go to bed. Joe was quite willing, and in a little while the two boys had retired for the night. Barry slept soundly, but his dreams were a strange mixture of trains, and boarding houses, and domes, and page boys, and Joe Harts.

He arose early in the morning very much refreshed. He learned that the House of Representatives would not meet until noon, but at the suggestion of his friend and mentor, he decided to go to the Capitol early in the day, in order to take the oath of office and to get acquainted with the duties of a page boy.

At nine o'clock he found himself in the office of the Clerk of the House of Representatives. The clerk was an elderly gentleman with a beard, and he treated Barry very kindly.

"I've heard of you, Wynn," he said. "John Carlton says that he wants us to take good care of you, and you can wager all you're worth we are only too glad to do anything that Carlton desires."

Barry bowed and blushed. He did not know exactly what to say to this tribute to his friend.

"I suppose," resumed the clerk, "that you are ready to be sworn in?"

"Yes, sir; I am."

"By the way, how old are you?" asked the clerk.

Barry looked at him in a startled way.

Was he to run up against a snag? His lips trembled in spite of himself.

"Is there an age limit for page boys?" he asked.

"Yes," was the response; "under the law, they must be over twelve years old."

Barry heaved a sigh of relief.

"I have just celebrated my fifteenth birthday!"

"Good," was the reply. "Now, if you will hold up your right hand I will administer the oath of office."

Barry held up his right hand impressively.

"Now," said the clerk, "repeat what I say."

"All right, sir."

Then the clerk recited, and Barry repeated the following form:

> "I do solemnly swear that I will support and defend the Constitution of the United States against all enemies, foreign and domestic; that I will bear true faith and allegiance to the same; that I take this obligation freely, without any mental reservation or purpose of evasion; and that I will well and faithfully discharge the duties of the office on which I am about to enter."

"It sounds very solemn, doesn't it?" commented Joe Hart.

"It sounds solemn and it is solemn," said the clerk. "It is the oath that everybody takes on entering the service of the United States Government. To break that oath, or to fail to fulfil its obligations would be little less than treason."

As they were turning away, Barry suddenly remembered something.

"Might I inquire how much pay I am to receive?"

"Certainly," said the clerk, "you will receive $2.50 a day while Congress is in session."

Barry could scarcely believe his ears. He had never dreamt that he would receive so much money. He mentally calculated what this would amount to in the course of a month, and then figured out how much money he would be able to send his mother after he had paid his board and refunded the money which Congressman Carlton had advanced for his railroad fare to Washington. The result must have been gratifying, because his face beamed like a new moon.

After this Joe took Barry through the Capitol in order that he might become familiar with the place. They passed through the corridors of the Senate Chamber and then down stairs where Joe pointed out the House and Senate restaurant.

"If you are sent to find a member and don't know where to go, always try the restaurant first," said the humorous one.

"Very well," replied Barry, seriously, "I will remember what you say."

"Now," said Joe, with an air of dignity, "I will take you up and introduce you to the Speaker of the House."

And so he did with all of the assurance in the world. The Speaker greeted Barry very kindly. He was a benevolent looking gentleman, without any pretense at greatness. He shook hands with the boy very cordially.

"I am glad to meet you," he said. "I am always glad to meet boys. You know," with a smile, "I was once a boy myself. If you want to be a success here, be attentive. Make up your mind that a member will not have to call you twice. Do that and you will be popular. Be economical, too. To save is good for all boys, and you should try to save most of your salary. I am an old man now and I am rich, but I can't help being economical, because it has become a habit with me. I might go to the finest hotel in the city and eat a heavy dinner, but I don't do it. I go over to a lunch place near the Capitol and have a sandwich and a glass of milk, and maybe a piece of pie, and I am perfectly satisfied. If you are economical when you are young, you will acquire all the money you need to keep you later on in life, and you can acquire it honestly, too, and that will make you feel very comfortable."

"I think I will make good," ventured Barry, shyly.

"My boy," said the Speaker, pointing a stubby forefinger at him, "if you are frugal and industrious, you are bound to succeed. These are two homely virtues that ought to be cultivated by every boy in the land, but unfortunately they are not. You will find as you go on in years that contentment does not consist of great wealth, but rather of few wants. Make up your mind that you will have regular habits; that you will take daily exercise; that you will be clean, and that you will be moderate in all things, and there is nobody in the world that can prevent you from being a success."

"I'm sure I'll do the best I can," said Barry.

"Of course you will," cried the Speaker, "but make up your mind that idleness is one of the seven deadly sins, and then you will be sure to be prosperous and happy."

He pulled out his watch and started away.

"I'm afraid that I'll have to be going, or I won't be able to get through with my work. If I can ever do anything for you, let me know."

After leaving the Speaker, Barry was presented to the head doorkeeper, who was to be his official superior. He did not waste many words with the boys.

"I suppose you're ready to go to work?"

"Yes," Barry said, "I am."

"Well, start in," he remarked, "and fill and clean the ink wells on the desks of the members."

Barry did not have any false pride, but this took him somewhat by surprise. Joe's talk had given him the impression that he was to be a statesman almost at once, but now he had come down to earth and was to fill ink wells. For the moment his hope of glory went glimmering, but he had the right stuff in him, and he was soon at work carrying out the orders of his chief. He did it well, too. He polished the ink wells until they were spotless, and he made sure not to drop any of the ink on the desks of the members. He was reassured also by the fact that one or two other boys were doing the same work. One of them, he noticed, was doing it very carelessly.

By this time the members began to assemble for the daily session. They strolled in the various doorways, singly and in groups. Some of them went to their desks and began writing; others stood in groups chatting and discussing subjects in which they were interested. The doorkeeper permitted no one to enter except members or specially privileged persons. The clock pointed to a few minutes of twelve. The Speaker ascended to the rostrum and took his seat back of the white marble desk, which was on a platform about four feet above the floor. To the right of his desk was the pedestal which bore the famous mace, the symbol of authority. It was a bundle of black rods bound with bands of silver and surmounted by a silver eagle. Barry was informed by his young friend that the Sergeant-at-Arms, in executing the orders of the Speaker, was required to bear this mace aloft before him.

Glancing up, the new page noticed a number of men coming into a gallery directly over the Speaker's desk. One of them he recognized as Felix Conway, the journalist who had spoken to him so kindly on his first arrival at the Capitol. He guessed directly that this was the press gallery for the reporters who were there to take down the proceedings of the House, and send them out broadcast to the millions of readers of the newspapers all over the United States.

While he was standing there staring at the gallery, he was brought to himself by a sound from the Speaker's marble desk. That official was tapping his gavel and calling the House to order. The proceedings began with a prayer by the Chaplain and then the clerk called the roll of members. He had scarcely finished when there were a flood of bills and petitions. For the next half hour Barry was kept busy running from one member to another, and receiving papers which he handed to the chief clerk, who stood at his desk directly beneath the platform of the speaker.

The members called the pages by clapping their hands, and if they did not get an immediate response, they clapped their hands two or three times in succession. The new page did the best he could under the circumstances, and he did it very well indeed. After this, bills which had been received before and ordered to be printed, were taken up in their order on the calendar and debated. In the midst of the talk one of the members in the rear of the House jumped to his feet and cried:

"Mr. Speaker, I move that the House do now adjourn."

Instantly the members were thrown into disorder. Loud voices came from all parts of the room. Men talked and gesticulated wildly. A member arose and protested against the motion. The Speaker looked at him calmly, tapped his gavel on the marble desk, and said:

"The motion to adjourn is not debatable."

In the midst of much excitement the clerk began calling the roll.

"Where's Warrington?" shouted one of the members to another, in a stage whisper.

"For goodness' sake, get Warrington before the clerk reaches the W's."

Barry heard this whisper and he acted on it at once. He shot out of the hall down the corridor until he came to the stairway which led to the House restaurant. A gentleman sat at a table eating a sandwich and drinking a glass of milk. He had been pointed out to Barry earlier in the day as Congressman Warrington. Barry rushed to him excitedly:

"Mr. Warrington," he cried, "they want you in the House at once."

This message delivered, he hastened back, followed by the member holding a half-eaten sandwich in his right hand. The boy turned into the hall of the House, the member at his very heels. The monotonous drone of the clerk's voice calling the roll could be heard.

"Mr. Warrington," he drawled.

Two members grabbed the bewildered Congressman as he entered the House.

"Vote 'no,'" they cried in chorus.

"I vote 'no,'" called the Congressman in a loud, clear tone.

A burst of applause followed the response. Almost immediately the voice of the Speaker could be heard.

"The motion to adjourn is lost," he said, "and the House will continue consideration of the General Land Bill."

An hour later the House adjourned and Barry was surrounded by a number of men who patted him on the head and bestowed all sorts of compliments on him. Presently the Speaker came along and said in an amused tone:

"Is this the boy that found Warrington?"

"The very same," was the response.

The Speaker patted him on the shoulder.

"You're the new boy I met this morning. You've started in right. You will be a great statesman some day."

"What was it all about?" said Barry to Joe Hart, as they journeyed homeward that evening.

"All about?" ejaculated the wise one, "why you're a hero, and you don't know it. If that motion to adjourn had carried, it would have defeated one of the most important bills that has ever been presented in Congress."

CHAPTER IV
VISIONS OF GREATNESS

When Barry Wynn and Joe Hart reached their Washington home they found Mrs. Johnson, the landlady, waiting for them. It did not take Barry long to discover that Mrs. Johnson was a very motherly person indeed, and one well calculated to take the place of his mother during the time that he was compelled to be away from home.

Mrs. Johnson, who was small of stature and very neat in appearance, was the widow of a clerk in the Treasury Department. She had been left with a large family and small means, but, being a capable woman, had been able to survive a crisis which would have shipwrecked the life of a weaker woman. Indeed, she had been able to educate her children through the profits of her enterprise. She had made a success of a boarding house, and in Washington this is saying a great deal.

Dinner was served at half-past six in a large, airy, and well-lighted dining-room. The atmosphere of the place was very pleasant and homelike. A big glass dish, filled with apple butter, stood in the centre of the table, and the mere sight of it filled Barry's mind with memories of home. The table was covered with clean linen and held a vase of freshly cut flowers. The dinner itself was good. The food was plain but wholesome, and the guests were all very friendly with Barry. There were nine or ten in all; three of the ladies were school teachers in the District of Columbia; two of the men were clerks in the Treasury Department, and another one held a position in the Patent Office. He was a very lively talker, and he managed to keep the guests at the table in a roar of laughter with the funny incidents which came to his attention in the course of the day's work.

After dinner most of the guests assembled in the large parlor and talked and chatted with all of the freedom that one usually finds in an affectionate family circle. One of the school teachers played the piano, while the Patent Office clerk, who had a good voice, treated his fellow guests to several selections from the popular songs of the day. It was all very chummy and very homelike, and Barry, who had feared that he might feel like a stranger in a strange land was, on the contrary, quite comfortable in his new home.

During the course of the evening Mrs. Johnson had a long conversation with him and asked him all sorts of questions concerning his home and his mother. She was very much interested in his replies and promised that when he returned home Mrs. Wynn would never have any cause to regret his selection of a boarding house in Washington. Barry's reference to his mother's widowhood brought tears to Mrs. Johnson's eyes.

"I had splendid prospects myself once," she said, "but the sudden and unexpected death of my husband dashed them to the ground and put me to the necessity of earning a living for myself and children. I thank a kind Providence that I have been successful, but the struggle has been a severe one and I know that it has aged me very much."

"I noticed a picture of President Garfield in the hallway," said Barry. "Did you know him?"

"He was one of our best friends," said the widow. "My husband was a classmate of President Garfield at Hiram College, and was one of his friends and supporters in nearly all of his political campaigns. After the General became President, one of his first acts was to appoint my husband a clerk in the Treasury Department. That was intended as a beginning. We both knew that he was to be promoted to a more important position as soon as possible, but Death intervened and that ended it all. However, the friendship of the President was deeply appreciated by John and myself. He called on us one day soon after he was inaugurated, and he was the same big-hearted, unaffected friend that we had known in Ohio. I could not help but think of him tonight at dinner. On the occasion of his call there was a big bowl of apple butter on the table. He called for a helping of home-made bread and then, in his big, boyish way, started in and ate the bread and the apple butter. He said that it reminded him of the days when he worked on the farm."

At about ten o'clock, during a lull in the conversation, Barry managed to leave the parlor unobserved and hurried up to his modest little bedroom. He had two reasons for doing this: the first was his desire to write a letter to his mother, and the second was the need which he felt for a good night's rest. He lit the gas, and was pleased to find a desk in the room with pen, ink and paper. On the first night he had only got a glimpse of his new quarters, and he now looked around and was delighted with the cozy appearance of his apartment. It was perfectly clean; the paint seemed fresh, and the paper was new. Two or three tastefully framed pictures adorned the walls, and an iron bedstead in the corner of the room was covered with a counterpane that was as white as snow.

Barry seated himself at the desk and started the letter to his mother. He had so much to tell that he scarcely knew where to begin, but presently his pen began to scratch the paper and he was fairly started. At intervals he paused and bit the end of the penholder, or scratched his head, or gazed up at the ceiling, in his efforts to think of the proper word that he should use in his correspondence. It proved to be quite a lengthy letter. He told his mother all that happened from the time he reached Washington until the moment he had begun his epistle. He told her about Congressman Carlton, Felix Conway, the journalist, Mrs. Johnson, his kind landlady, and last, but not least, he related all that he was able to tell about Joe Hart, his fellow page.

After he had concluded he sealed and stamped the letter and carried it out and dropped it in a letter box at the corner of the street. He was about to prepare to go to bed on his return, when his attention was attracted by a modest-looking shelf in one corner of the room. His love for reading caused him to make a close examination. He found that one shelf contained a copy of the Bible, a set of Shakespeare in one big volume, a history of the United States, a Congressional directory, a condensed history of the nations, and a life of James A. Garfield, the martyred President of the United States. It seemed to Barry, young as he was, that these six volumes might be said to contain a liberal education in themselves.

Every one of them was worth careful perusal, but boy-like, he turned to the life of Garfield and began to skim it over. Before he realized it he was thoroughly absorbed in the volume. He read of the boy who was born in poverty, and who, through his own efforts, had risen to the highest position in the gift of the American people. The story was a reality to Barry Wynn. He could see young Garfield when he was scarcely twelve years of age, driving in the cattle, carrying wood, hoeing potatoes, building fires, and doing whatever else there was for willing hands to do. He could see the future President lying flat on the floor of the barn, reading the life of Napoleon, and he could see that same boy exclaiming to his mother with youthful enthusiasm: "Mother, when I get to be a man, I'm going to be a soldier," and then later on in the book, he read about the boy, after he reached manhood, who became one of the bravest soldiers in the Civil War.

But the most interesting part of the magic volume, so far as Barry was concerned, were the pages that told of the future President of the United States working as a mule driver on the narrow banks of the canal. Young Garfield once thought that he would like to become a pirate, but as his reasoning powers became stronger, he discarded this romantic idea and settled down to the unpoetic work of everyday life, and although he did not become a pirate, he managed to secure employment on a canal boat in his own State, and during his first night's work became involved in a quarrel with a bully of a deck hand, and thrashed the fellow within an inch of his life. After that, James A. Garfield went to school for a while, and finally became a student in Hiram College, Ohio. Later he was promoted to the proud position of a teacher in the institution in which he had started as a pupil. Barry read on and on, following his hero from one position to another, until he reached the Presidency, only to become the victim of an assassin's bullet.

Finally Barry reached the last page of this wonderful book, and he laid it down with a sigh of relief and yet of regret. He happened to glance at the small clock which was ticking on the mantle. It pointed to fifteen minutes of two in the morning. It startled the boy. He had no idea that the time had passed so rapidly. He undressed quickly and put out the light, and was just about to jump into bed when he heard the sound of footsteps in the hallway. He opened his door cautiously and as he did so he saw Joe Hart going into his room on the other side of the corridor. Barry was too sleepy to feel very inquisitive, but in a vague sort of way, he thought that Joe Hart was certainly keeping very bad hours.

After that he threw himself into bed. He lay thinking for some time. The thought of the book he had just read kept running through his mind. One sentence in it came to him as clearly as if it had been committed to memory. It was an extract from an address which Garfield had delivered to the students at Hiram College. The President, on that occasion, had said:

"Poverty is uncomfortable, as I can testify, but nine times out of ten the best thing that can happen to a young man is to be tossed overboard and compelled to sink or swim for himself. In all my acquaintance I never knew a man to be drowned who was worth saving."

Barry felt, in an incoherent, drowsy way, that he had been tossed overboard. He wondered whether he could sink or swim, but before the answer came he was sound asleep.

CHAPTER V
A WINK AND A NOD

At breakfast the next morning Mrs. Johnson informed Barry that Congressman Carlton had sent a message to the house requesting that he call at his office as early as possible that day. The boy hurried through his meal and in a few minutes was swinging down Pennsylvania Avenue on his way to the Capitol. Despite his hurry, his eye lingered on the various edifices which were springing up on either side indicating the beautiful city in store for future generations. Indeed, the charm of Washington always remained fresh in Barry's mind.

He learned that Mr. Carlton had his headquarters in the new office building of the House of Representatives, which was but a stone's throw from the Capitol. In a few minutes the boy was tapping timidly at the door opening from one of the marble corridors of the substantial building. There was no response and he turned the knob and walked in. He found that he was in a suite of rooms, and through the door he could see the Congressman seated at his desk in another room.

He paused a moment before announcing himself. John Carlton, absorbed in the work before him, presented an interesting study. His smooth-shaven face was most attractive, and even in the privacy of his room he did not lose that appearance of authority which is carried so well by men who mix in the practical affairs of life. A half smile hovered about his lips, but at that very moment a kind of sadness showed itself in his eyes. He was a combination of the man of imagination and the man of the practical world. As he laid down the letter which he had been reading, he raised his eyes and saw the boy standing in the doorway.

"Come in, Barry," he exclaimed. "Come in and let me get a good look at you."

The new page walked in and stood before the desk very modestly.

"I suppose," said the Congressman, "that you are feeling very big this morning?"

Barry looked at him in surprise.

"Why, no," he said, "I don't quite understand you, Mr. Carlton."

The legislator lay back in his chair and laughed with undisguised enjoyment.

"I am glad of it. I am heartily glad of it," he said. "It proves that there is one person in Washington who is not likely to be afflicted with the awful disease which goes down here under the name of 'swelled head.'"

The boy's eyes were globular with wonder.

"I don't suppose you know what I am talking about, Barry, do you?"

"No," was the simple response, "I do not."

"Well, I'll tell you," said the Congressman, speaking very slowly. "You came mighty near making yourself famous in the House yesterday. Your alacrity in bringing Warrington to us was the means of saving a very important bill. If he had not come at the time he did, the measure would have been delayed and probably beaten. As it was, you helped us to win the day. The measure, that is now sure of success, gives the President of the United States the right to withdraw certain public lands for the benefit of future generations. It is a part of what is popularly known as the Conservation Movement."

"I am glad that I was useful," said Barry.

"You are not half so glad as I am," said the Congressman, "and I am delighted to know that you take it so sensibly. You simply did your duty, and if you continue to do your duty in this modest sort of way I know that you will be a success."

The telephone bell rang and Mr. Carlton answered it. As he hung up the receiver the boy said:

"I was told that you wanted to see me this morning."

"Yes," said Mr. Carlton, drumming on his desk with his finger tips. "Barry, can you work the typewriter?"

"Yes, sir; and I have a good knowledge of stenography, too."

"Well," was the response, "I suppose it may sound a little sentimental, but I have written the bill to make an appropriation for the new Naval Repair Station at Cleverly, and I want you to run it off on the typewriter. You know very well the feeling I had towards your father, and I would like to be able to say that you wrote the bill for this big improvement in your native town. It's not much, I know, but I thought you might like it."

Barry's eyes were glistening. He spoke eagerly:

"I think it's just fine, Mr. Carlton, and I want to assure you that I appreciate it very much indeed."

Without further ado, Mr. Carlton gave him the manuscript copy of the bill, and Barry, going to a typewriter in a corner of the room, began to transcribe the document. While Barry was at work on the machine Mr. Carlton began the task of going through his mail. It was no easy job, for there were probably a hundred letters on his desk and that merely represented one day's crop. He ran an opener through one envelope after another and remarked casually as he did so:

"I am waiting for my secretary, Barry. I don't know what keeps him so late."

At that moment the door opened and the tall, spare form of Felix Conway, the journalist, entered the room. Mr. Carlton pretended to frown:

"You're late, sir."

"Yes, sir," was the reply, with mock humility. "I'm sorry to say, sir, that I overslept myself, sir."

At this both men burst into laughter. Barry was so interested and so surprised that he forgot to run his typewriter. Mr. Carlton turned and noticed the look of amazement on the boy's face.

"It's all right, Barry," he exclaimed. "Mr. Conway is not actually my secretary, but he has consented to act the part for the next few weeks. My real secretary is ill, and I was in dire need of someone who understood legislative and departmental matters when Mr. Conway was good enough to step in and help me out in the emergency."

"Yes," laughed the journalist, "and in helping you out, I will only be repaying, in a small measure, the many kindnesses you have shown me since I came to Washington."

Barry worked slowly on the typewriter, because he was anxious to have his first piece of work as accurate as possible, and besides the fact that the Congressman and Mr. Conway were engaged in conversation distracted him more or less from the task in hand. He could not help but overhear the talk that passed between the two men.

For instance, Mr. Carlton pulled a letter from an envelope and after reading it, passed it over to the volunteer secretary.

"Here's a man who wants a pass from Boston to Cleverly," he said. "Tell him the new Interstate Commerce law forbids the issuance of passes, and that if the railroad granted his request, the officers of the corporation would be liable to a fine and imprisonment."

The journalist laughed at the sarcasm of the statesman.

"I guess the constituent who wrote that letter must have been asleep for the last two years," he commented. "He don't seem to have kept up with the procession."

Mr. Carlton nodded in assent and handed another letter to the newspaper man.

"Here's a communication from a constituent in the country. He applies for seed. Send it to the Agricultural Department with my endorsement."

Mr. Conway noted the instructions on a corner of the envelope, using a sort of shorthand that was all his own.

After this came a letter from an inventive genius, who had a flying machine which he wished to have adopted by the United States Army. It was referred to the Secretary of War. There were twenty or thirty letters asking for information of bills that were pending. They were laid aside to be answered in their turn. Finally they reached a communication from a poor widow who was applying for a pension. Mr. Carlton carefully deciphered the uncertain handwriting and then said to his assistant:

"Felix, I wish you would take this up in person with the head of the Pension

Bureau. I think the woman deserves consideration. Her husband served his country in its hour of need, and this nation is too great to neglect those who have risked their lives in its service."

"Have you anything else?" asked the young man.

"Yes," was the reply, "here is a five-page letter."

"What is it?"

"It is from a man who wants me to get the Army to purchase a new kind of saddle that he has constructed."

"What shall I say to him?"

"Tell him that I'm not a salesman."

Felix Conway gathered up the pile of letters and went into an ante-room for the purpose of dictating suitable replies to a waiting stenographer. The Congressman, in the meantime, looked at Barry with a benevolent smile, and said:

"Barry, you have just had a glimpse of a part of the work that falls to the lot of an active member of Congress. You will see from this that the job of being a statesman is not a sinecure. In fact, it is very hard work, and I am sorry to say that some of the voters look upon the members of Congress as errand boys, whose sole time should be devoted to carrying messages to the various heads of Departments."

"That is not all the work, either?" asked Barry.

"Not by any means; the most exacting work that falls to the lot of a member is that of discussing and digesting proposed legislation when it comes before the various Committees of the House."

By this time Barry had finished making his copy of the bill providing for the new Federal building in Cleverly. He handed it to Mr. Carlton, who read it over very carefully. He made one or two minor corrections, and then said he was very much pleased with the work.

The Congressman laid the bill down on the desk, and was about to turn to some other work when there was a tap on the door and two gentlemen entered the room. One of them was a little man, dressed in black, and wearing a white linen bow tie. He wore side whiskers and had a peculiar expression. Barry looked at him the second time, and then discovered that his face was really conventional, and that its unusual expression was caused by the queer drooping of the eyelid of the left eye. The man who accompanied him was a tall, sallow-faced, loose-jointed person, who gazed steadfastly at the floor. Mr. Carlton arose at once and greeted both men heartily. The little man gave him a quick grasp of the hand in reply, while the sallow-faced person said "Good morning" without looking at his host. They talked in whispers for a few minutes and then Mr. Carlton called Barry over to him.

"Barry," he said, indicating the little man in black, "I want you to meet the Hon. Jesse Hudson. Mr. Hudson is one of my colleagues, a member of the House of Representatives."

Then, turning to Hudson, he said:

"This boy comes from my native town. He is the son of one of my oldest friends. I have made him a page in the House, and if you ever get an opportunity to help him, I wish you would do so."

Congressman Hudson took Barry's hand with that quick, convulsive movement which seemed to be one of his characteristics, and said:

"Glad to meet you. If you ever need anything call on me."

After this Barry was presented to the sallow-faced man, who proved to be Mr Joel Phipps, who was the clerk to the Committee on Naval Affairs.

As the general conversation was resumed, Barry withdrew and took his seat in the corner of the room. Just as they were about to leave, Congressman Carlton said suddenly:

"By the way, Hudson, I am going to introduce a bill in the House in a few days to appropriate a million dollars for a Naval Repair Station at Cleverly. I know that you are a member of the Committee on Naval Affairs, and I wish you would help me to put this measure through. We need it and it's a just and proper appropriation."

Mr. Carlton stooped down to pick up a paper, when Congressman Hudson, turning to the clerk, said:

"Oh, we will help you with it, won't we, Joel?"

As he said this he deliberately winked at the sallow-faced man, and in return he nodded and replied:

"Yes, certainly we will help Mr. Carlton."

And after that they both withdrew. As the door closed Mr. Carlton turned to the boy and said:

"Those are good people to know, Barry. Both the Congressman and the clerk have considerable influence in legislation and they have the power to either help or hurt you."

"I suppose they have," responded Barry.

He longed to tell his friend of the sign that had passed between the two men, but he was afraid that if he mentioned it, Mr. Carlton might think that he was very presumptuous. Besides that, he thought that possibly he might have been mistaken. However, he said finally, with a great deal of diffidence:

"I can't say, Mr. Carlton, that I am very much attracted by either of those men."

"Well, Barry," said the Congressman, a little coldly, "you must take people as you find them in this world, and not as you think they should be."

All the same, Barry did not relish the recollections of the wink that had passed between the two men.

CHAPTER VI
HUDSON STRIKES A SNAG

Joe Hart went to great pains to show his growing regard for Barry. He instructed him in his work as page and pointed out various ways of making himself useful to the members of Congress. One of these ways was to familiarize himself with the numerous public documents issued by the Government. Every member, said Joe, had calls for bills and reports from time to time, and if a page boy could tell a member where to put his hands on a certain paper at a given time, the value of the page would be immensely enhanced in the eyes of the member. Barry took the advice to heart and determined to profit thereby.

One morning, when Barry was on his way to the Capitol, it occurred to him that it would be a good thing to call upon Congressman Carlton and ascertain whether there was anything he could do for him. He found the Congressman at his desk in his office immersed in a great heap of correspondence that was before him.

"Good morning, Mr. Carlton," said Barry. "I don't want to disturb you. I just dropped in to ask whether there was anything I could do for you before I went to the House."

The Congressman paused for a moment and looked at Barry, while he tried to recall some particular thing that he was very anxious to have done. It came to him quickly.

"By George!" he exclaimed; "you're the very boy I want. There's a big pile of Committee Reports in the next room that I would like to have sorted out and piled up in regular order. I have no doubt that most of 'em are only fit for the furnace, but I'm afraid to destroy any of 'em for fear that I may burn the very documents I need."

Barry's eyes sparkled.

"I'll be delighted to undertake the job, Mr. Carlton," he said. "It's something I'm interested in, anyhow."

The Congressman stared at the boy.

"Interested? What do you mean?"

"Oh, nothing; except that Joe Hart tells me that I should become familiar with public documents of all kinds in order to increase my usefulness to members of Congress."

The Congressman clapped his hands on his flat top desk with quiet delight.

"Bully for you! If you continue in this way there's no telling where you may land. You know every boy in this country has a right to aspire even to the Presidency."

Barry reddened with embarrassment.

"Oh, Mr. Carlton, I never dreamed of anything like that."

"Of course, you haven't. No healthy boy ever really expects to reach such a great honor as that, but you can aspire to other big things. One of the oldest members of the Senate served in the position that you hold now, while a half dozen members of the House were pages at your age."

"Well," said Barry, with boyish confidence, "I am certainly going to try to amount to something."

"Very good," said the Congressman, and he dismissed the boy with a wave of the hand. "Now, you go into the other room and see what you can do with that old junk."

Barry went to work with a will. He found that he had a pretty big job ahead of him, but he went at it systematically and resolutely. He took the reports according to dates and piled them up in little heaps in the order of the months and the years in which they had been printed. Occasionally he was attracted by the heading of some of the documents, and in one or two instances he was so interested that he read the reports from beginning to end. In this way several hours passed, and looking up at the clock, he discovered that it was twenty minutes of twelve. He realized that he had just about enough time to get over to the House and to report for duty. He was about to go in and speak to Mr. Carlton when he heard the door open and someone came into the Congressman's room. The gentleman spoke to Mr. Carlton. Barry recognized the voice at once. It was that of the Hon. Jesse Hudson.

"Hello, Carlton," said Hudson, "when are you going to introduce that bill for a Naval Repair Station in your town?"

"I'm going to do it soon," said Carlton. "It's pretty nearly in shape for presentation."

"Good," was the response. "You can count on my help in getting it through the Committee. If you meet with any obstacles, just come to me and I will be glad to give you a lift. Are you going over to the House?"

"Not for a few minutes," was the response. "I've a couple of telegrams that I want to send out before I leave here."

"All right; I'll go over alone then. By the way," he continued, as he paused at the door, "I've got a measure coming up today, and I'd like you to help me get it through."

"What is it?" asked Carlton.

"It is known as the Garner claim. A family in my district had their property destroyed during the Civil War. It seems that the Federal troops occupied their house and barn and when they got through with them they were practically ruined."

"What is the bill for?" asked Carlton.

"It is to reimburse the heirs for their loss. It calls for an appropriation of $96,000. It should have been paid long ago!"

"Who are the heirs? The children of the claimant?"

"No, not the children, but some of their relatives."

"Is it all right, Hudson?"

"Sure, it's all right."

"Well," was the slow response, "if it's a fair bill, I suppose I will have to turn in and vote for it, but I don't like to support these claims for damages without knowing all about them."

"Oh, it's all right," was the confident response; "I'll see you later. Good-bye."

As he swung out of the room Felix Conway, the journalist, walked in.

"Hello, Felix," exclaimed Carlton. "You're just the man I want to see. You know everything, don't you?"

The newspaper correspondent shook his head and said, smilingly:

"No, not everything—nearly everything."

"Well," said Carlton, "I'd like to know what you can tell me about the Garner claim. It calls for an appropriation of $96,000 to repay certain heirs of the Garner family for property destroyed during the Civil War."

The journalist looked blankly at the Congressman.

"Blest if I know a thing about it. It's the first I've heard of it."

"I'm awfully sorry," said the Congressman, "because I'm anxious to get some of the facts in the case."

As Felix Conway left the room Barry Wynn emerged from the little apartment where he had been sorting out and piling up the public documents.

"Mr. Carlton," he said, timidly, "I couldn't help overhearing your conversation with Mr. Hudson and Mr. Conway. You were speaking to them about the Garner claim."

"I was, indeed," was the response. "You don't mean to tell me that you know anything about it?"

"Yes," was the hesitating reply, "I know a little about it."

"When did you hear of it?" was the surprised question.

"The first I heard of it was when Mr. Hudson came in," replied Barry, "but I read about it an hour ago."

"Read about it?"

"Yes; when I was going through those old papers I found a report from the

HUDSON STRIKES A SNAG

House Committee concerning the Garner claim."

Carlton's eyes glistened.

"Where is it? Where is it? Let me have it."

Barry went into the other room and came out again in a few moments with a small public document.

Mr. Carlton seized it eagerly and read the heading:

> "Report of the House Committee concerning a claim of the heirs of Samuel Garner for damages sustained to their property during the War of the Rebellion."

That was enough for him. He sat back in his chair and read the document from start to finish. It was an adverse report. The document was ten years old, but the Committee that had been entrusted with the investigation of the matter reported that the claim was a very doubtful one, and that in any event the heirs should be compelled to go into court for the purpose of obtaining relief.

Carlton stuffed the report in his inside pocket, and slapping Barry on the back, said:

"Barry, you've done me a great favor."

Ten minutes later Carlton was at his desk in the House of Representatives, and Barry was standing by the desk of the chief clerk, waiting for the proceedings of the day to begin. At the stroke of twelve the Speaker brought his gavel down on the top of the marble block before him and called the House to order. The Chaplain made a brief prayer, and then the members from all parts of the great hall began rising in their places and presenting bills. The pages ran up one aisle and down another, with bills fluttering in their hands, rushing and laughing and tumbling about like so many little imps. Barry kept his eye on Mr. Carlton, and when that gentleman rose in his seat, made a mad rush in his direction.

"The Gentleman from Maine," called the Speaker, in a loud tone.

Whereupon Mr. Carlton presented a number of minor bills. Barry was at his elbow, and taking the papers hurried to the Speaker's platform and had the satisfaction of seeing the bills referred to the various Committees of the House.

After his measures had been safely disposed of, John Carlton made a search for Jesse Hudson. He had determined to inform him that he would not support the bill in favor of the Garner heirs. When he reached Hudson's seat, he found that gentleman busily engaged in conversation with another man, but that did not deter him. He broke in between the two and said:

"Hudson, I'd like to speak to you for a moment."

The other frowned and waved his hand, saying:

"You will have to excuse me. I am very busy at present."

Carlton walked back to his own seat very much dissatisfied. Fifteen minutes later he noticed that Hudson was disengaged and walked over in his direction.

The moment Hudson saw him, however, he slipped out of his seat and left the House. The inference was obvious. Hudson was trying to evade Carlton. The business of the House continued for about half an hour and then the clerk, in stentorian tones, announced that the next business in order was the consideration of the bill granting relief to the heirs of Samuel Garner. Hudson was in his seat. Carlton grasped the opportunity and was by his side in an instant.

"Hudson," he said, "I've been trying to reach you all morning to tell you that I can't support—"

"Don't talk to me now," cried the other, impatiently. "Don't you see that I'm busy?"

"You can't be too busy to talk business," was the angry retort. "I want you to know that I can't support your Garner bill. I'm simply telling you this, so that you can be under no false impressions in the matter."

"Why, what's the matter?" asked Hudson, simulating a look of surprise.

"Well, I'm sorry to say the matter is that I don't think it's a fit bill to vote for."

"What do you mean?"

"Just what I say. After you left me this morning, I got a report of the House Committee that was made nearly ten years ago, and it seems very conclusive to me—so conclusive that I've made up my mind to fight your bill."

"Oh, you're splitting hairs," cried Hudson, in a tone of annoyance.

"Well, you can give it any name you like."

"But, see here, Carlton," cried Hudson, eagerly, "I won't ask you to vote for it if you don't feel like doing so; but promise me one thing."

"What's that?"

"Don't make a speech against it. Don't oppose it openly. It's backed by some of the most important men in my district—men who can make or break me."

"I can't make any more promises," said Carlton, and he moved slowly back to his own seat.

In the meantime the House was giving close consideration to the Garner claim. Near the end of the debate Jesse Hudson arose and made a strong speech in favor of the passage of the bill. The sentiment of the House seemed strongly for the heirs. If the members had taken a vote after Hudson's speech, the chances are that the bill would have become a law. But just at that critical moment John Carlton rose in his place and was recognized by the Speaker.

"Mr. Speaker and Gentlemen," he said, with great deliberation, "before the House votes on the bill that is now pending, I desire to read a copy of the report that was made on this very claim by a Committee of this House ten years ago. The members can find the document by referring to their files, volume II, page 1072."

There was a lifting of desk lids and a scurrying of page boys, and every member in the House seemed seized with a desire to get a copy of the document in question. In the meantime John Carlton read the report in slow, measured tones. As he concluded he said:

"Mr. Speaker, I have no comment whatever to make upon this report. I merely call it to your attention. For my own part, after reading that report, I cannot see my way clear to vote for this bill."

It was as though a bomb shell had been thrown into a quiet, peaceable gathering. Members stood on their feet, and talked, and gesticulated, while the Speaker vainly motioned the members to their seats. Presently, the calling of the roll brought order out of chaos. Hudson ran from one member to another imploring them to vote for his bill, but it was too late. When the vote was announced it was found that the Garner claim had been overwhelmingly defeated.

Shortly after that the House adjourned. Hudson, in leaving his seat, almost bumped against John Carlton. He looked at him with a malignant frown, and said bitterly:

"You're a fine fellow to promise to support a bill!"

"I withdrew my promise before it was too late," said the other one, quietly.

"Yes, you withdrew it, but you made me a promise all the same."

"I didn't make any promise."

"I say you did!"

"Well," said Carlton, easily, "there's no use wrangling over it. It's all over now."

Hudson doubled up his fist, and shaking it at his adversary, said:

"It's not all over. Not by a long sight! Every dog has his day, and I'll have mine sooner than you think!"

Carlton laughed.

"There's no use borrowing trouble," he said, lightly. "The dog-days won't be here for some time yet."

As they passed out of the door into the corridor of the Capitol, a third member came up to Carlton and said:

"John, were in the world did you dig up that report?"

"Oh," was the response, "it was pulled out of a pile of old junk in my office."

"How did you have the patience to go through that stuff?" asked the inquirer.

"I didn't," was the reply. "It was discovered for me by a very bright boy, named Barry Wynn."

CHAPTER VII
BARRY STUMBLES

As Barry Wynn and Joe Hart were walking down Pennsylvania Avenue the following morning, Joe suddenly turned to his friend and exclaimed laughingly:

"Barry, this is the happiest day of all the glad new year!"

Barry looked at Joe blankly.

"Why; what's happened? Have you good news?"

"Bully news."

"What do you mean?"

"Can't you guess?"

"No, I can't."

"Why, you old hayseed, this is pay-day."

Barry's face beamed. Naturally he looked forward with great pleasure to the first money he had ever earned. He voiced his feelings to Joe:

"The work here has been so pleasant that I actually lost count of the days. I never dreamt that I'd been in Washington for a month."

"Well," said the practical one, "you'll know all right when you go up to the cashier's office this morning."

The experienced boy led the novice to that part of the Capitol building where the pages received their checks. Barry had to sign the pay-roll and after that swore that he had rendered the service for which he was about to be paid. He was handed a nice, bright, crisp check drawn to the order of Barry Wynn against the Treasurer of the United States. He looked at it with ill-concealed curiosity and then gave a gasp of delight. The check was for sixty-eight dollars. He had worked a little less than a month, but the sight of the voucher for so much money gave him a sense of elation that he had never felt before.

With Joe still acting as mentor, he cashed the check, and on reporting for duty to the Sergeant-at-Arms, was gratified to learn that he had been given leave of absence for the day. Joe also, by some occult influence, managed to be excused. Barry's first move was to call on Congressman Carlton and to inform him of the amount of money he had received. Mr. Carlton was delighted, but somewhat taken aback when Barry handed him a ten-dollar note.

BARRY STUMBLES 33

"What's this for?" he asked, somewhat stiffly.

"It's the money you advanced for my railroad fare to Washington."

The good-natured man burst into a hearty laugh. He clapped his big palm on Barry's shoulder and said jovially:

"Just put that away. You'll have lots of use for it. The money I sent you was a present."

"But, Mr. Carlton," insisted Barry, "mother made me promise that the first money I received should be used to pay you back the ten dollars you sent me for my ticket."

"Nonsense! I don't want it."

"But, I must give it to you," persisted Barry. "If I don't my mother will never forgive me."

Mr. Carlton accepted the note somewhat reluctantly.

"By the way," he said, reaching into his pocket, "here's an old wallet that I have no more use for. Now that you have become a man of wealth it may be a convenient thing for holding your money."

Barry took the gift and thanked Mr. Carlton.

"Now, Barry," said the statesman, "I don't want to overburden you with advice, but if I were in your place my first move would be to pay your landlady for the board that is due her, and then give her a week or so in advance. After that lay some money aside for your personal use, and then skedaddle to the postoffice and make out a money order for the balance in favor of your mother. She will appreciate it more than words can tell."

"I'll do it," was the fervent response.

"All right. Good-bye, and good luck to you."

As Barry left the Capitol building he came in contact with Joe Hart, who had also cashed his warrant. The two boys proceeded to their boarding house and both of them paid Mrs. Johnson the money that was due her, together with an advance payment towards the coming month.

"Now, what are you going to do?" asked Joe.

"I'm going up stairs and write a letter to my mother," said Barry. "I want to enclose a money order to her and get it off in the mail as soon as possible."

"All right," said Joe. "I'll wait for you, and then we'll go down town together. Or, if you want to," he added, as an after consideration, "you can walk right over to the postoffice building and write your letter there."

Barry adopted the suggestion and the two boys left the house together. As they turned the corner of the Treasury building, the clock in the neighborhood struck the hour of twelve.

"Jiminy!" exclaimed Joe, "it's time to eat."

The remark put an idea into Barry's head.

"Joe," he said, "this is pay-day; let's celebrate!"

"Celebrate?" echoed the other.

"Yes. I want you to take dinner with me today."

Joe looked at his friend in silence for a moment, and then something suspiciously like moisture glistened in the corner of each eye.

"Barry," he said, "I'll go you—it's the first time in my life that I ever remember anybody asking me out to dinner."

Barry was determined to do the honors becomingly, so he sought out a first-class restaurant and ordered dinner for two. The linen was white and the dining room splendidly furnished. An orchestra, hidden behind a cluster of palms, enlivened the occasion with the popular songs of the day. The meal was complete; it began with soup and ended with ice cream. To say that the two boys enjoyed themselves would be putting it very mildly indeed. They felt as though they were in an enchanted fairyland. The fact that Joe's legs were too short to touch the floor, and that he swung them to and fro on the chair did not detract from his dignity in the least, and when the head waiter, who had seated them with all the pomp and ceremony which can only be employed effectively by a head waiter, and addressed them as "gentlemen," their cup of happiness seemed full to overflowing, but the limit had not yet been reached. After the meal was finished and the attendant placed a finger bowl in front of each of the boys, the giggling and the whispering and the mischievous glances that passed between them would have been sufficient to have gladdened the heart of the most confirmed pessimist. But the crowning act of all came when Barry, after having paid the bill, majestically tipped the waiter. From that moment he was a superior being in the eyes of Joe Hart.

After leaving the restaurant they resumed their walk down Pennsylvania Avenue. The events of the preceding hour had raised them both in their own estimation. They strolled along very proudly, indeed, and did not feel a bit ashamed when three Justices of the Supreme Court passed them on the street. Senators and members of the lower House of Congress they looked upon as very ordinary beings indeed; in fact, when the President shot by in an automobile on his way to the White House, they regarded it—as it was in fact in Washington—as an incident of everyday life. It was about two o'clock by this time, and they were half way down the avenue when Barry's attention was attracted by a large sign advertising a moving picture show.

"Joe," he said, with proper dignity in his voice and manner, "I want to do this treat right. Let's take in the picture show."

Joe did not require a second invitation. In a few minutes they had paid their dimes and were ushered into the seats of the little temporary theatre. In the rush of hurrying in, the two boys had become separated, although they managed to obtain places in the same row. A woman with a market basket was on one side of Barry, while a burly fellow, with a red necktie, was on the other. Presently the place was filled and the lights were turned down. The films began to operate upon the canvas. The scene represented an explosion in a coal mine. It was very vivid and very lifelike. There was a flash of lightning and then a low rumbling sound which marked the beginning of the disaster. At the most interesting stage of the performance Barry felt himself being crowded by the man who sat next to him. The fellow acted so roughly that Barry protested.

"Stop pushing me!" he cried.

"Oh, I beg your pardon," was the polite reply, "I didn't intend to annoy you. It was an accident."

The moment that Barry had spoken he was sorry. It was probable, he thought, that the man had leaned against him unintentionally and he regretted his resentment. He wondered whether he should not apologize. The lights went up in a minute or two, but Barry found, to his surprise, that his neighbor with the red necktie had already departed.

The two boys wended their way out to the street together and were glad to get in a whiff of fresh air. They made their way slowly towards the new postoffice building on Pennsylvania Avenue, and after selecting a convenient desk, Barry began writing his letter to his mother. The work of composition was aided by Joe Hart, who, at intervals, offered many unique and unsolicited suggestions. Finally the missive was completed and Barry exclaimed:

"Now for the money order. I'll go over to the window and buy it."

He reached into his pocket for the wallet in which he had placed his money. His hand slid into vacancy. A look of grief overspread his face.

"What's the matter, Barry," cried Joe; "are you sick?"

"No," said Barry, "I'm not sick. The pocketbook's gone!"

The two boys stood looking at each other speechlessly for many moments. Presently Joe spoke:

"Do you think you had it when you went into the moving picture show?"

"I *know* I had it then."

"Well, the answer's simple—you've been robbed!"

For the time being Barry felt as though the universe had gone to pieces and lay in chaos at his feet, but after awhile he came to his senses, and at the suggestion of his friend, the two of them started to retrace their steps from the postoffice to the moving picture theatre. They had gone about two blocks when Joe Hart suddenly exclaimed:

"Look. What's that in the street?"

Barry followed the glance of his friend and saw a red wallet lying on the asphalt, in front of a Pennsylvania Avenue store. He ran over and picked it up. It was his own. He opened it and looked into one side of the wallet. It was empty. He turned to the other and looked in, and to his satisfaction, found a solitary ten-dollar bill. He showed it to Joe Hart.

"What do you think of it?" he asked.

"I think the man that stole the wallet took the money out of the one side and thought that that was all there was in it. Then he threw the wallet away to get rid of it."

After that the boys walked back to the postoffice, where Barry bought a postal order for ten dollars. He destroyed the letter which he had written to his mother originally, and began the composition of a second one. It was a slow and painful task.

"I don't know just what to say," he said. "I've told mother that I got sixty-eight dollars for my month's pay and I've explained how I used part of it in paying Mr. Carlton and another part in settling what I owe Mrs. Johnson. I'm sending her the other ten dollars, but she'll wonder what I've done with the rest. I haven't got the nerve to tell her that I've lost it. What would *you* do?"

"Don't know," said Joe, aimlessly.

"Maybe it would worry her," said Barry. "I'll just—"

"I say, Barry," interrupted Joe, with his queer expression; "do you know the best way?"

"No."

"Just tell her the truth—tell her exactly what happened."

And Barry did.

CHAPTER VIII
AN UNEXPECTED MOVE

Mr. Carlton now had his Naval Repair Station measure in good shape and he considered the time ripe for its introduction in the House of Representatives. One morning, when the Speaker called for new bills, he handed in the typewritten document on which all of his ambitions and his hopes were pinned.

"The bill presented by the Gentleman from Maine is referred to the Committee on Naval Affairs," announced the Speaker.

Barry, who had carried the precious draft from the Congressman's desk to the Speaker's platform, could not resist the opportunity of whispering a word of exaltation to his patron.

"She's in at last, Mr. Carlton," he said, "and you ought to feel proud and happy."

The Congressman sighed.

"She's in, Barry, but that's only the first step in the battle."

"But it's a good bill," insisted the boy, earnestly, "and it has been approved by the Navy Department."

"Not yet, but I hope it will be soon," corrected Mr. Carlton.

"Then it will pass, sure."

The statesman smiled at the boy's enthusiasm.

"I'm not so positive of that," he said. "I've known many a good measure to go to a Committee and after that never see the light of day again."

Nevertheless John Carlton felt very optimistic over the Naval Repair Station bill. But he had been in Congress too long to permit himself to become affected with the political disease known as "over-confidence." He had prepared the draft of the law with great care. He knew of cases where the omission of a word, or the dropping of a comma, had destroyed the effect of important legislation.

Also, he had sounded a number of members of the Committee on Naval Affairs and found that they were well disposed toward the bill. He intended to push the legislation solely on its merits, but he knew that in Congress, as elsewhere, the intelligent and industrious representative is apt to outstrip the man who does not possess these homely but essential qualities.

Felix Conway was in the House when the bill was offered and he immediately began the preparation of a dispatch to the two evening newspapers that he represented. Both were in the district affected by the location of the Naval Repair Station in Cleverly, and both were enthusiastically in favor of the proposition. It was at the suggestion of Mr. Conway that these newspapers had avoided any premature announcement of the project. He feared that such advance publicity might produce a host of rival cities, all claiming to have available sites, for the proposed station. Now that the bill had actually been offered, it was featured in both of Mr. Conway's newspapers with big headlines and diagrams of the intended improvement. That night he wired it to the big New York newspaper which he also represented at Washington.

This was the beginning. Both the Congressman and his friend realized the importance of developing a public sentiment in favor of the bill. They knew that the site was an ideal one. It remained for them to impress that fact upon the members who would be called on to pass upon the bill. The mere introduction of the bill was a big piece of news, and it was printed broadcast in all of the newspapers of the country. But the greatest interest, of course, was displayed by the Eastern press.

Mr. Carlton made sure to attend the first meeting of the Committee on Naval Affairs after the introduction of the measure into Congress. After brief debate the bill was referred to the Secretary of the Navy for his consideration. He in turn passed it over to a Committee of experts, with a request for an early report. In the meantime day after day passed and Mr. Carlton watched anxiously to see if the people of any other locality would come forth with a site. But time went by and none appeared and he felt greatly relieved.

In the meantime events were moving rapidly. The Board of Experts visited Cleverly and made a careful inspection of the site of the proposed station. Mr. Smithers, the President of the Board of Trade, offered his services to the visitors and answered questions with such confidence and pointed out the advantages of the place so convincingly that the Board of Experts unanimously favored the bill. The Naval men realized that the Government had an opportunity that should not be neglected. They returned to Washington well pleased with their trip and in a few days sent a glowing report to the Secretary of the Navy, who, in his turn, forwarded it to the Committee on Naval Affairs.

John Carlton was delighted. Things were progressing better than he had expected. Felix Conway wrote a series of letters for his morning newspaper, showing that the location of the station at Cleverly would not only be good for the Government, but would also give permanent employment to five or six hundred men. He was enthusiastic and he elaborated on his theme. He even went so far as to declare that it meant a new era of prosperity and that not only the city and State, but the nation would share in the good times. This brought sharp retorts from newspapers out of the Cleverly zone and one or two of them hinted that Cleverly was not the hub of the universe in spite of the eloquent outbursts of Felix Conway.

Barry was now in the thick of events. Mr. Carlton had made an arrangement with him by which the boy was to give all of his time to him when he was not engaged in his duties as page. Barry was surprised at the number of things he was

AN UNEXPECTED MOVE

able to do. First he went through the newspapers and clipped out all editorials and news articles bearing upon the proposed Naval Repair Station. There were many hundreds of these, and the young page arranged them in large envelopes according to the views expressed therein. Those that favored Cleverly were placed in one package; those that opposed it, in another. He planned to keep the indifferent comments by themselves. Strange to say, none of the newspapers were indifferent. A few were unfriendly to the suggested site, but the great majority of the articles and the editorials agreed that Cleverly was the natural and desirable spot for the Naval Repair Station.

Resolutions, petitions, memorials, letters and telegrams came pouring in on Congressman Carlton commending him for presenting the bill, and urging him to carry his work to a successful conclusion. He felt well pleased with the situation. The new Naval Repair Station promised to make him popular as well as important. One of the members of the House congratulated him on his prominence in the public eye:

"It's very nice," he admitted, "but I'm not letting it take me off my feet. You know a political leader who receives bouquets today may get brick-bats tomorrow."

Finally the House fixed a date after which it was decided that no new bills could be introduced. Mr. Carlton put in some anxious hours. He wondered if something might not occur at the last moment to upset his plans. But the day arrived and passed and no new Naval Repair Station bill had been presented. Mr. Carlton was overjoyed. It seemed almost certain that his measure was to have smooth sailing.

The following day a meeting of the Committee on Naval Affairs was called for the purpose of transacting general business. Among other things the Clerk of the Committee read the report made by the Board of Naval Experts on the proposed Repair Station at Cleverly. It was clear and it was convincing. The words were music to the ears of John Carlton. But, as the clerk finished, Mr. Collins, one of the members of the Committee, arose and said:

"Mr. Chairman, I now request that the clerk read the bill making an appropriation for the construction of the Naval Repair Station."

Congressman Carlton was on his feet instantly.

"What is the purpose of having it read now?"

"I wish to offer a little amendment to the bill," was the reply.

"All right," said the unsuspecting member.

The bill was read, and as the clerk concluded, Mr. Collins rose and said:

"I move to strike out the portion of the bill fixing the location of the station at Cleverly, and to insert the words, 'Green Island.'"

Half a dozen members were on their feet at the same time, all claiming recognition at once. The Chairman nodded to Mr. Carlton and the others sat down.

"Mr. Chairman," cried the Congressman, "this is a most astounding amendment. It changes the whole purpose of the bill. It is not fair to do this at the last moment without giving the members a chance to consider what it means."

Mr. Collins flushed.

"The gentleman has no right to say that. It is a reflection on me."

"I have no desire to reflect on the member," said Mr. Carlton, "but I'd like to know the meaning of the amendment."

"I'm not prepared to discuss it now," confessed Mr. Collins. "In fact I presented the amendment by request."

"Then you're willing to postpone consideration for the present?"

"Yes."

"For how long?"

"Well, say two weeks."

And so it was agreed.

After the meeting Mr. Carlton went to his fellow member:

"See here, Collins; who are you representing in this matter?"

"My constituents, of course."

"No; but you said that you presented the amendment by request."

"That's true."

"By request of whom?"

The member smiled. He did not relish the aggressive manner of the gentleman from Maine. He answered rather ironically:

"I'm not prepared to give you that information—at least not for the present."

John Carlton was greatly chagrined at the turn of affairs. He was prepared for open opposition, but how could he fight a foe who remained in the dark? Green Island was not in Collins' district. So it was plain that the amendment was inspired by someone else. Carlton tried to find out who this one was and failed. Felix Conway was called into consultation and the two men went to the Congressman's office, where they discussed the question for more than an hour. But when they finished they were no nearer a solution than in the beginning. Just as they arose the door opened and Barry Wynn came into the room. He was breathless.

"Mr. Carlton!" he cried. "Mr. Carlton!"

"Well, what is it?"

"I've found out who got Mr. Collins to offer that amendment."

Both men were on their feet. They spoke simultaneously.

"Who was it?"

"It was Congressman Hudson," replied the boy.

CHAPTER IX
ON THE TRAIL OF JOE HART

Barry had obtained the information which he had given his patron, in the most commonplace way. After the session of the Committee, he was sitting in the corner of the room talking to Joe Hart, when Jesse Hudson and Mr. Collins came along talking very earnestly. Hudson said to the other:

"Much obliged for offering that Green Island bill. I'll do as much for you some day."

That was enough for Barry. He realized the importance of this disclosure and hastened to tell Mr. Carlton. He met with some delay in locating him, but finally found him in his own room with Felix Conway, where he made his startling announcement.

Ten minutes after exploding this verbal bomb, Barry started home with Joe Hart. On the way it occurred to him that he was beginning to have a genuine affection for the mischievous page boy. Joe was as full of pranks as an egg is full of meat, but Barry was quick to learn that none of his tricks were cruel or mean. He was simply overflowing with animal spirits. He was capable also, quick to know what was required of him, and prompt to act. Joe Hart was not prepossessing to look upon. He had a thick thatch of red hair, a freckled face, and stub nose, and a pair of blue eyes that gazed upon you with a look of appealing inquiry and the innocence of an angel.

"Joe," said Barry one day, "you must have been a terror at school."

"Yes," replied Joe, with a comical twist of the mouth, "whenever any of the boys were bad, the teacher lathered me. He said he couldn't go wrong."

"The Sergeant-at-Arms of the House is very fond of you," suggested Barry.

"He must be," replied Joe, "he scolds me so much."

Barry had been in Washington three weeks, when he came home one evening about eleven o'clock and found Mrs. Johnson, his landlady, in tears. He was very much exercised at this unexpected sight. It was as though he had found his own mother crying.

"Why, what's the matter?" he asked.

"It is all about Joe Hart," she said, lifting a corner of her apron and furtively wiping away the tears.

"Why, what about him, Mrs. Johnson?"

"Well, you know he is like yourself: he is like a son to me. His mother placed him in my charge, and in a measure I am responsible for his conduct. Now, you know it would break her heart if he would go wrong or get into bad habits."

"Oh, he's all right, Mrs. Johnson."

"I wish I could feel so sure," she said. "I've been anxious about that boy for a long while. He is getting careless. He is spending all of his money and he stays out late at night."

"Well, I stay out myself sometimes, Mrs. Johnson."

"Yes," she said, "but I know where you are, and besides, you have never been out later than eleven o'clock. Why, one morning it was one o'clock when he got home, and you see tonight, it is already past eleven."

"Well, I think you'll find it's all right," said Barry, soothingly.

"But I must know that it's right," she persisted. "Won't you help me?"

"I'd be glad to do anything I could for you."

"Well, you can help if you want to."

"How?"

"By finding out where Joe Hart has been spending his nights."

Barry raised his hand in protest.

"Oh, Mrs. Johnson, I couldn't do anything like that."

"Yes, you could," she replied, with a doggedness that some women can employ so effectively.

"But I couldn't," he reiterated. "Joe 'd never forgive me."

The tears left her eyes at this response and a look of anger replaced them.

"Well," she said, angrily, "I can pry into his business and I am going to, and if you won't help me, I'll get somebody that will!"

Barry went to bed that night feeling very uncomfortable. He had his own suspicions concerning Joe Hart, but he did not have the courage to give voice to them. Besides it distressed him very much to feel that he had incurred the displeasure of his motherly landlady. All the next day the incident bothered him, and more than once he found himself looking anxiously at Joe and wondering whether it would not be a good thing to ask his young friend to explain the cause of his unusual conduct. But he did not, and the feeling of his discomfort weighed heavily upon him every hour of the day.

That night at dinner Barry noticed that Joe was very much preoccupied in his manner. He bolted his food and kept looking at the clock with an unnatural anxiety.

"What's the matter, Joe?" asked Barry. "Have to go out?"

"Yes."

"Where?"

Joe seemed confused for a moment and then said hastily:

"Oh, it don't make any difference."

A few minutes later Joe went to the door and looked out, and then came in again and began drumming on the table cloth.

"What's the weather like?" asked Barry, in an attempt to make conversation.

"Looks like rain," replied Joe, aimlessly.

Barry could stand this no longer. He walked to his young friend and said in a determined voice:

"Look here, Joe Hart, what do you mean? You say it looks like rain, and the sky's full of stars. You don't know what you're talking about. What's on your mind?"

Joe's freckled face reddened to the ears. He showed more confusion than Barry had ever known him to display before.

"I was thinking of something else," he mumbled. "I guess you're right about the weather. It doesn't look like rain at all."

Barry walked away very much dissatisfied. It was evident that Joe was trying to deceive him, and he did not relish that. Presently the boy came over to him very shyly.

"Barry," whispered Joe, in a sort of awe-stricken voice. "Have you got four or five dollars to spare?"

Barry hesitated.

"It's only until pay-day," said Joe, eagerly. "I'll get my check in a week and I'll be sure to pay you back."

"It's not that, Joe," said Barry, gently. "I'd be willing to give you every penny I've got in the world, but I hate to see you waste your money."

"Oh, it won't be wasted," he cried.

Without another word Barry put his hand in his pocket and pulled out a pocket-book, reached in and lifted out a five-dollar note and handed it to the other.

"You're a bully fellow," exclaimed Joe, in his old happy-go-lucky, care-free manner. "I knew you wouldn't go back on an old pal."

"Of eight weeks' standing," said Barry, drily.

Joe's eyes danced with delight.

"That's a long while in these days of fierce competition."

Five minutes later the door slammed and Joe had disappeared. At the same moment Mrs. Johnson came to Barry.

"I overheard your conversation, and it has distressed me more than I can explain. I feel more than ever that it is necessary to find out what this boy is doing with his money and where he spends his nights."

Barry looked at her helplessly.

"I don't see how I can help you, Mrs. Johnson."

Her eyes sparkled.

"Yes, you do. I have made up my mind that I will look after him and I have also made up my mind that you are going to help me."

Barry laughed, feebly.

"Well, if that's the case," he said, "I guess I might as well take my orders."

"Well, I want you to go after him right away. Don't let him see you, but find out what he does with that money."

"Oh, Mrs. Johnson," said Barry, "I couldn't do that."

She began to weep and in a moment or two threatened to become hysterical.

"I must know," she exclaimed. "I must know, and if you don't go after him I'll get my bonnet and go myself!"

After this there was nothing for Barry to do but put on his hat and follow Joe Hart. The boy had a start of three or four blocks, but Barry could see him passing under an electric light near the end of the Treasury Building. They went block after block until they reached the poorer section of the city on the outskirts of the railroad tracks. Presently Joe stopped at a fruit stand and began examining the stock of the Italian who presided over the place. In a few moments he had purchased a basketful of peaches, pears, and plums. At this stage of the pursuit Barry's better feelings came to the surface again and he resolved that he would follow Joe no farther. He turned off into a side street. Somehow or other he lost his way. Coming out of the other end of the street he almost ran face to face into Joe Hart. But the little page was so absorbed that he did not notice his friend. Joe walked up to a small, mean-looking house in the middle of the block, facing a large, vacant lot. Barry hid behind the trunk of a convenient tree. Joe rapped on the door and a poorly-clad, pale-faced woman responded. Her face brightened at the sight of Joe.

"Good evening, Mrs. Lewis," cried Joe, in his cheeriest voice, "how are the children getting along tonight?"

"They're better, thank God," she cried, fervently. "The doctor says that the crisis passed yesterday and they will be on the mend in a few days."

"I'm mighty glad to hear it," said Joe.

"It's very kind of you to come here," continued the woman; "and I'm sorry I can't ask you in."

"Don't mention it. I'm a busy man, and haven't much time to spare. Here's a basket of fruit. Here's the prescription you wanted last night, too."

"May Heaven bless you," cried the woman, the tears coming into her eyes. "I don't know how in the world I can ever repay you for your goodness to us."

"Don't mention it," cried Joe, brusquely. "Here's a five-dollar bill. You may need it."

"Oh," she said, "I can't really take this."

"You must!"

"But I won't be able to give it back to you."

"Well," said Joe, with a laugh, "we'll put that up to Danny. We'll make Danny pay me when he gets better."

And the next moment Joe had started off in the darkness. Barry came out from his hiding place. The woman saw him.

"Are you looking for Joe?"

"Yes; has he gone?"

"Yes," she said, "he has just gone." And then, looking at him inquiringly, "Do you know him?"

"Yes, ma'am; he's my chum."

"Well," she said, "if you know him you know an angel in disguise. My Danny says that and Danny ought to know."

"Danny?" said Barry, inquiringly.

"Yes," she replied, "my boy, Danny Lewis. He is head of the local messenger boys in the district telegraph office. He was taken sick two weeks ago and the doctor said it was typhoid fever. Someone had to take his place at the office, and when Joe Hart heard of it he volunteered to act as substitute. For more than a week he has been acting as page in the House during the day and chief of the telegraph boys at night. He did it to keep Danny from losing his position. You know these things are mighty uncertain. Now the week for Danny's night shifts is passed and everything is safe, but Joe didn't stop at that. He knew we were poor, and he has been buying food and fruit almost every night."

The strange lump that came into Barry's throat prevented him from making any reply. But his hand was perfectly free, and when he put it into Mrs. Lewis' she found that he had left another five-dollar bill in her palm.

Half an hour later, as he turned into the street where Mrs. Johnson's boarding house was located, he almost collided with Joe Hart, who was coming in another direction. He looked at him very fixedly and said in a stern voice:

"Where have you been?"

"I've been out."

"That don't answer my question," said Barry, severely. "I want to know where you've been spending your nights."

"Oh, nowhere in particular," said Joe, hastily, and then, in an endeavor to turn the subject, he said:

"How do you like your work at the Capitol?"

"It's none of your business how I like my work," laughed Barry, "but it is my business to tell you that you've been discovered!"

"Discovered!" echoed Joe.

"Yes. Caught, captured, found out! Don't you know the meaning of the English language?"

"Yes, but I don't know what you're talking about."

"I'm talking about the way you've been spending your time the last two weeks. I know all about you."

"How do you know?"

"Well, I saw you tonight and know all that you did."

For an instant Joe threatened to become belligerent. He doubled up his fists and came towards Barry in a menacing way. Then he reconsidered himself and his hands dropped listlessly to his sides. He spoke in a reproachful way:

"I think that was mighty mean of you, Barry Wynn."

"I think so, too," confessed Barry. "I'm ashamed of myself all right, but Mrs. Johnson was worried, and Joe—Joe, I'm mighty proud of you."

Barry, as he spoke, put his arm around Joe's shoulder, but the boy pushed it away. His face was flushed and he looked embarrassed.

"Say, Barry," he said finally, "I want you to make a solemn promise to me."

"What is it?"

"Never mind what it is. I want you to say that you will do as I say."

"All right," said Barry, finally; "I'll promise. What is it?"

Joe looked the picture of humiliation. His eyes were on the ground and he spoke pleadingly:

"Barry, it's just this. I want you to promise me that you'll never mention this business to the other boys at the Capitol."

"Why?" asked Barry.

"Because, I'd never hear the last of it. Those fellows would just guy the life out of me."

Barry, his heart swelling with a new and peculiar sensation, made the promise.

"I WANT YOU TO MAKE A SOLEMN PROMISE TO ME"

CHAPTER X
SUSPENSE

It became evident in the course of a few days that the amendment to the Naval Repair Station bill was to be pushed vigorously. In fact a great deal of sentiment in its favor developed in the most unexpected places.

Mr. Carlton had been under the impression that a large majority of the members of the Committee were for the Cleverly site as against any other, but he learned that he was mistaken. Some of the members declared themselves openly in favor of the Collins amendment; others said that the new proposition was deserving of very careful consideration.

Naturally this worried the Congressman. He spent many anxious hours and days in trying to strengthen his own position. Curious to state no one now seemed to care anything about Cleverly. On the other hand there was wide-spread interest in Green Island. There was a reason. The amendment in favor of Green Island had just enough mystery about it to pique the curiosity of the law makers.

The fact that Jesse Hudson was behind the bill was also significant. It meant that there was at least a chance of its passage. Hudson was not in the habit of enlisting in losing fights. He was one of the best known members of the House. He had served eight consecutive terms. He was resourceful; he was industrious, and he knew the methods of procedure by heart. Besides that he had a great many friends. And that made him a foeman worthy of any man's steel. Some persons pretend that friendship has ceased to exist in the world. It is not true. The poorest man has some friends. Others—even though they be unworthy—have many friends. Friendship is a great asset to any man. It is invaluable to the man in public life. Carlton realized this fact. He knew that Hudson had served so many men in his day that some of them would want to serve him now. And the member from Maine felt very, very anxious about his favorite piece of legislation.

Two of the things against the Green Island project were its apparent lack of support from the people of that locality, and the fact that it had not been endorsed by the Secretary of the Navy. Under ordinary circumstances the lack of these two requisites would have been sufficient to defeat any bill. In this case, however, they did not seem to count much. One of the reasons was that the land at Green Island was offered to the Government for a much lower price than had been fixed for the site at Cleverly.

"How can you explain that away?" asked the Secretary of the Navy of Mr. Carlton.

SUSPENSE 49

"Easily; it's not worth one-fourth as much."

The cabinet officer laughed.

"I like your positiveness."

"I can prove every word I say."

"Maybe you can."

"There's no 'maybe' about it, Mr. Secretary. I know what I'm talking about."

"The other fellows say the same thing," suggested the Secretary.

"See here," cried the Congressman, "you don't intend to indorse this Green Island scheme, do you?"

The Secretary became serious.

"Certainly not. I have already placed the seal of my approval on the Cleverly site. I believe this is the very best location we could get on the Atlantic Coast. But, that is merely my say-so."

"It's sufficient," protested Carlton, stubbornly.

"I hope so; but you mustn't underestimate the shrewdness of the fellows who are against you."

"You wouldn't let it go through, would you?" cried the Congressman, in alarm.

"Not if I could help it, but the thing might get beyond my control."

"How?"

"Well, I suppose you know that we are in urgent need of this Naval Repair Station?"

"I'm sure of it."

"You know, in fact, that we must have it at once."

"Yes."

"Well, suppose these fellows pass the Green Island bill and then have Congress adjourn."

"Well?"

"Picture the position in which I would be placed. If I ask the President to veto the bill, I am put in the attitude of killing a project for which I have been fighting."

"But not in the same place."

"No; not in the same place. But the difference in the desirability of the sites might not be considered sufficient cause for killing the bill after it comes from Congress."

"I see."

"Of course, you see. Now, it's up to you to defeat the Green Island scheme, and after that to pass the Cleverly bill."

"It's a pretty big contract to give to one man."

The Secretary laughed.

"Your shoulders are broad. Besides, I'm sure you must have some good friends."

"No one ever had better ones," was the fervent retort.

"Well, enlist them in your cause. Good-bye, and good luck to you," were the final words of the Cabinet officer.

John Carlton left with a smiling face, but down in his heart he had grave misgivings. As he entered the hall of the House he met Barry Wynn.

"Well, my boy," he said with outward cheerfulness that never deserted him, "what's new?"

"A great deal," replied the young page. "The members have been handing in petitions this morning in favor of placing the Naval Repair Station at Green Island."

"Many of them?"

"Hundreds and hundreds of them. Why it looked like a snow storm of white papers. They came from all parts of the House."

"Did you say they were all on the same kind of paper?"

"No, I didn't," retorted Barry; "but now that you speak of it, they were all on one kind of paper."

Mr. Carlton nodded his head knowingly.

"It's just as I thought. This is not a natural outburst from the people. It's a scheme—a set-up job."

Barry looked at him helplessly.

"Can I do anything?" he asked, finally.

The Congressman was plunged in thought. Finally he looked up at the boy:

"Yes," he replied, "everybody can do something, Barry," he added, "we've got to stir up Cleverly as it has never been stirred up before. We must have a delegation of citizens come here and present their claims to the members of the Committee on Naval Affairs; we must get in touch with everyone that is worth his salt, and we must have telegrams, letters and petitions fairly rain down upon the members from now until the meeting of the Committee."

The shower came and it was helpful. Also, Mr. Smithers sent a telegram, saying that he was organizing a delegation of leading citizens and that they would reach Washington in a few days. Barry, acting under the direction of Mr. Carlton, sent a number of letters to men who would be likely to assist in agitating the superior claims of Cleverly. One day, after a number of these petitions had been presented in the House, Mr. Carlton happened to meet Jesse Hudson.

"Hello," said the rival, who was still smarting over his defeat in the Garner claim, "you seem to be busy."

"This is my busy day," retorted Carlton, with imperturbable good humor.

"What are you trying to do, advertise Cleverly?" persisted Hudson.

"Incidentally," replied Carlton.

"You know that's all you'll ever get out of it," sneered Hudson. "You know you'll never get that Naval Repair Station."

"No; I don't know that," said the man from Maine; "but I'm glad to get the news from such a distinguished authority. You know you are such a reliable prophet. You remember you said the Garner claim was sure to pass."

Hudson was too angry to reply to this sally. He stalked down the hall with his chin in the air, looking as if he could bite nails. Carlton, on his part, hurried to the office of the Secretary of the Navy. He was anxious to know whether there was anything new in the proposed naval station legislation. The Secretary was not in, but his chief clerk said he would be glad to give the Congressman any information he might have.

"What can you tell me about the proposed station?" asked Carlton.

"Nothing, except that a delegation called here yesterday in the interest of Green Island."

"They did?"

"Yes, sir; and they presented a set of blue prints showing how much the Government would gain by locating the repair station at that point."

"Blue prints don't mean everything," commented the Congressman.

"That's what the Secretary said, and he referred them to the Board of Experts that visited Cleverly."

"Did they go to Green Island?"

"No; they have no authority from Congress to examine the site."

"But they scrutinized the plans?"

"Yes."

"What was the verdict?"

"That, leaving out geographical considerations, the land at Green Island would make as good a location as that at Cleverly."

Mr. Carlton left the office of the Secretary of the Navy in a very thoughtful frame of mind. He realized that the opposition was making progress, and that his own cause was losing ground.

CHAPTER XI
DISCORD AND DEFEAT

One morning, while Barry was on his way to the Capitol, he passed a popular second-class hotel, known as the Olympic. Quite a crowd had gathered around the entrance to the house and inside the parlor a band was playing the popular airs of the day. Barry hesitated for a moment. Then he turned and went in to satisfy his curiosity. Over the entrance to the double parlor of the hotel was a sign reading: "Headquarters of the Citizen's Committee of Green Island."

He realized that he was in the camp of the enemy. Also, it came to his mind that the backers of the Green Island scheme had resolved to stake the success of their enterprise upon a spectacular campaign. This method of procedure was not new to Barry. He had attended several political conventions and he knew more than one candidate who had accomplished by brag and bluster what would have been impossible through the use of reason. The citizens of Green Island were numerous and noisy. Most of them were puffing away at big black cigars. Some of them, in the words of a witty Hibernian, "were at the bar of the House, pouring red liquor down their English, Irish and French channels." But about it all there was an air of aggressive excitement. "I'll tell you," cried one citizen, whose high silk hat looked like a misfit, "I tell you the people of Green Island do not ask for this Naval Repair Station. They demand it!" This outburst was greeted with loud and prolonged cheers.

When Barry reached the House he reported what he had seen to Congressman Carlton. That gentleman seemed greatly impressed:

"This means that we must be on guard day and night," he said. "Sometimes important legislation is put through with a rush."

For the first time since the project was broached, Mr. Hartman, the Congressman whose district included Green Island, now came to the front in defense of the bill for a Naval Supply Station. Carlton met him in the lobby that day:

"Why, Frank," he said in an injured tone, "I never knew that you were going to father a Naval Repair Station bill at this session of Congress."

The legislator looked at him in silence for a moment and then burst into a laugh.

"To tell the truth, I didn't know it myself, John."

"Well, what does it all mean?"

DISCORD AND DEFEAT 53

"Blest if I know."

"But you're backing the bill?"

"Yes, of course, I am. But to be entirely frank with you, I didn't know a thing about it until it was introduced as an amendment to your bill in the Committee on Naval Affairs! It interested me then because it was in my district. It interested me still more because it had been presented by a member outside of the district. I was passive. I didn't support or oppose the bill. I was like the man from Missouri. I wanted to be shown. But yesterday a delegation arrived from home. They included some of my constituents. They asked me to support the bill. I protested against the manner of its introduction, and they admitted that that was a mistake which they regretted. So there you are. On the face of it the proposition is all right. It is supported by men who have supported me. So I suppose I'll have to work and vote for the bill."

"You don't seem to be working very hard."

"No harder than is necessary," was the languid reply.

Carlton was pleased, but not entirely satisfied. The Green Island proposition was really stronger than it had been at any time since its presentation. Three Congressmen were openly committed to it, and a large and enthusiastic delegation of citizens was "boosting" it from early in the morning until late at night. Carlton hoped that the Committee from Cleverly would reach Washington soon. He felt the need of a counter demonstration.

That afternoon he received notice that a meeting of the Committee on Naval Affairs would be held the following day for the purpose of acting on the Green Island amendment. This was short notice, but the Congressman started to work at once. He made a canvass of the Committee, and the result left the matter in doubt. Many of the members said that if the Cleverly proposition was the only one before the Committee, they would gladly promise to vote for it. The Green Island amendment, however, put a different aspect on the question. Most important of all the land at that place was offered to the Government for one hundred dollars per acre.

"What is the price of your site by the acre?" asked one of the members.

"About one hundred and twenty dollars," replied Carlton.

"You see it's higher than Green Island."

"But it's better," was the retort.

"That's to be proven. At any rate, why don't you reduce the price of yours?"

Carlton smiled and shook his head.

"That's impossible."

"Why?"

"Because it would be a confession that it had been made too high in the beginning. Besides the property owners have fixed the price at the assessed value of the land. Many of them could get more for their property. But they've been public spirited enough to shade down to the lowest point for the sake of having the station located at Cleverly."

"Then your people won't offer any other inducements?"

"I'm pretty sure they will not. We want the station very much, indeed, but we want it on its merits."

That night at the boarding house Joe Hart invited Barry to go out with him.

"Where?" asked the boy.

"I've promised to go over and see Danny Lewis."

"Sure," said Barry, "I'll be glad to go with you."

He remembered with pleasure Joe Hart's kindness to the Lewis family, and he wanted to meet Danny, the messenger boy, concerning whom he had heard so much from his fellow page. They found Danny at home, and they spent the evening with him in the cosy sitting room of the little house. Danny proved to be a bright, intelligent chap, with a sense of humor and Barry liked him very much. Presently he recounted some of the odd experiences he had undergone in the service of the telegraph company.

"I suppose they keep you very busy," suggested Barry.

"Rather," smiled Danny, "and lately it's getting so that we don't have a minute to spare."

"Why?"

"Well, for one thing, those Green Island boomers keep us on the jump."

Barry was interested at once.

"I suppose they have a great many telegrams," he said.

"Suppose is no word for it," replied the boy; "it's a stern reality."

"They're hustlers," conceded Barry.

"Yes, and they're fighters, too."

"Fighters?"

"Yes; fist fighters."

"What do you mean?"

"Why, when I was delivering a telegram this morning, the chairman of the delegation got into a dispute with one of the other men and it ended in a rough and tumble fight."

Barry was absorbed.

"What was it about?"

"Oh, this fellow accused the chairman of freezing him out; said his land was good as any other, and if they didn't take him in, he'd raise trouble—only he used a stronger word than trouble."

Barry was on his feet now and had his hand on Danny's shoulder.

DISCORD AND DEFEAT

"Did—did you hear the fellow's name?"

"Sure; his name was Gaskill—they called him Billy Gaskill."

"Boys," said Barry; "I hope you'll excuse me. I've got an important engagement."

Joe laughed.

"You're getting to be an important man."

Barry smiled back as he reached for his hat.

"If you knew what this meant, you wouldn't make fun of me, Joe," he said.

Joe waved his hand magnanimously.

"It's all right, Barry. You can do as you please, and no questions asked."

From the house of Danny Lewis the page boy hastened to John Carlton's hotel. It was late, and the Congressman was preparing to retire.

"Hello, Barry," he cried, "what in the world do you want at this hour of the night?"

The page boy, in a few quick, jerky sentences told him what he had heard from Danny Lewis. Moreover, he said he had learned that Billy Gaskill was still at the Olympic, and most important of all that he continued in a bad humor.

Congressman Carlton went to the telephone and called up the office of Felix Conway.

"Can you come here?" he asked.

"If you need me."

"I've got some big news for you."

After that the legislator insisted that Barry should go home.

"You go and get your rest," he said. "There's nothing more that you can do for me tonight. See me the first thing in the morning."

The following morning each of the newspapers served by Felix Conway contained an article denouncing the Green Island bill for a Naval Repair Station as a sordid scheme, backed by a combination of unscrupulous land speculators. It did not mince words, and it caused a genuine sensation at the Capitol. Mr. Hartman, the Congressman from the Green Island district, was amazed. He never had much faith in the bill, but he had supposed that it was legitimate at least. He hurried to the Olympic Hotel and presented himself to Dwight Whalley, the chairman of the Green Island boomers.

"See here, Whalley," cried the disturbed Congressman, "have you read these articles about the Green Island site?"

"Have I?" echoed the Chairman, "I should say so. We've all read them."

"Well, what have you got to say?"

"Say? Why that I'm as mad as a hatter; we're all mad as hatters."

Mr. Hartman waved his hand wearily.

"I don't care anything about feelings. I want to know whether the story is true."

"True?" he repeated. "Surely you don't intend to pay any attention to a sensational newspaper article."

"Don't you?"

"No; certainly not."

"Very well; now, I know what to do."

"Mr. Hartman; Mr. Hartman!" called the Chairman.

But the Congressman was already out of sight. Before noon that day a statement appeared, over the signature of Mr. Hartman, in which he disclaimed all further interest in the legislation affecting Green Island. This added fuel to the fire. Before the Committee met that afternoon nearly everyone in and around the Capitol appeared to be interested in the fight over the Naval Repair Station.

Carlton was on hand very early. Prior to the meeting he held several whispered conversations with Felix Conway. He was here, there and everywhere. There was an air of aggressiveness about him that boded no good for the opposition.

"He seems ready for the battle," suggested one of the Committeemen to another.

"Yes," was the reply. "He's ready to fight at the drop of the hat."

The Committee was called to order, and the clerk read the Green Island amendment as offered by Congressman Collins. The moment he finished Jesse Hudson got the floor:

"I move that the amendment be adopted," he said.

Carlton was on his feet instantly.

"I think," he said, in purring tones, "that the gentleman has not had the opportunity of reading the articles that appeared in this morning's newspapers, otherwise I'm sure he would not favor this legislation."

"I've no time to read sensational newspapers," snapped Hudson.

"Then I'll have to enlighten the gentleman," said Carlton, still very polite.

"How?"

Instead of answering Hudson, the man from Maine looked about him inquiringly:

"Is Mr. William Douglass in the room?" he called.

In response a square-jawed man advanced to the desk of the Chairman.

"Gentlemen," said Carlton, looking about him smilingly, "Mr. Douglass lives on Green Island, and with your permission I want to ask him one or two questions about the Green Island site."

"This seems irregular," protested Hudson.

"It may seem irregular," was the retort, "but you'll find it will be all right."

"What do you hope to demonstrate through Mr. Douglass?" asked the Chairman.

"That this whole Green Island proposition is a land speculation scheme," retorted the Congressman sternly.

The members all looked up at this grave statement. Everyone was paying the closest attention.

"Now, Mr. Douglass," said Carlton, "you're well acquainted with this property, are you not?"

"I know every inch of the ground."

"Do you know the owners of it?"

"I did know the old owners."

"What do you mean by the old owners?"

"I mean that the entire property has changed hands during the last few months."

"Since it first became known that the Government intended to build a Naval Repair Station?"

"Exactly."

"Now, Mr. Douglass, these new owners are offering this property to the Government for one hundred dollars an acre. What did they pay for the land?"

"Less than twenty-five dollars an acre."

"That's all," said Carlton, promptly.

There was a hum of excited voices. Hudson protested that the price of the land had nothing to do with the case, but his argument was lost in the din. A ballot was called for, and the Green Island amendment was overwhelmingly beaten, only two votes being recorded in its favor.

CHAPTER XII

SMITHERS TO THE RESCUE

For twenty-four hours after the defeat of the Green Island bill John Carlton was kept busy responding to congratulations. Barry Wynn was one of those who ventured to express his joy to the Congressman.

"I'm awfully glad you've won the fight," said the boy.

The statesman beamed on the youngster.

"You mean well, Barry," he exclaimed, "but I'm afraid you're a little previous."

"But you beat them."

Mr. Carlton nodded.

"Yes, we defeated their bill, but we haven't passed our own!"

"But you will."

"I hope so, but I know we're going to have a terrific battle. Hudson and the others are bitter over their defeat, and they'll move Heaven and Earth to beat the man from Cleverly."

The session was now drawing near its close, and Mr. Carlton knew that if he was to get his bill through, he would have to get action by the Committee. Accordingly he had a day fixed when the members agreed to hear the citizens of Cleverly. That accomplished, he wired Mr. Smithers to be sure and have his committee in Washington at the time appointed. The caution was heeded, for when the great day arrived, Mr. Carlton received word that the delegation had reached the Capitol city. Barry tried to locate them but failed. He did not know at what time they reached Washington, or where they were domiciled. The only thing he could do was to possess his soul in patience. The public hearing was scheduled for two o'clock in the afternoon in the Committee room, and Barry felt that they would be likely to appear there before the hour indicated.

He was not mistaken. Ten minutes before the time the delegation filed into the office of Congressman Carlton. Postmaster Ford headed the party, and directly behind him were Mr. Smithers, Hiram Blake, and several other prominent citizens of Cleverly. Mr. Carlton received them cordially, and then Barry went around to them, one by one, shaking hands with a fervency that could not be mistaken. The sight of the familiar faces stirred him until every drop of blood in his body seemed to tingle with delight. The sense of elation was greater than words could properly describe. The sight of their dear old faces was like a whiff of ozone from the ocean

SMITHERS TO THE RESCUE 59

to a person parched with the heat of summer.

He had so much to say, and they had so much to say, that none of them knew where to begin. The consequence was a genuine hubbub of voices and a babble of sounds. Hiram Blake, as his relative, naturally claimed his attention. These two talked in whispers for quite a while and the things that Barry learned from his uncle made him very happy indeed. His mother was well and contented, and pleased with the progress that he was making in Washington.

After he had finished his talk with his uncle, Barry turned his attention to Mr. Smithers. He had to shake hands with him again and again in order to convince himself that it was really the old schoolmaster himself in the flesh that stood before him. Mr. Daniel Smithers, it might be said, parenthetically, was a different person in Washington from Mr. Smithers in Cleverly. He was dressed neatly and in good taste, and had indulged in the luxury of a shave and a hair cut. Mr. Smithers, like most men of his class in the east, was not only highly educated, but was a man of great capacity, and from the moment he landed in Washington he had been fairly drinking in knowledge. He absorbed facts and figures and information generally as a sponge absorbs water. While the other members of the party had been indulging in the pleasure that comes from viewing monuments and paintings, Mr. Smithers had been making the rounds of the departments, and picking up odd bits of information concerning the government of the country, that he was to retain in his wonderful head the rest of his life. He visited the Treasury, Patent Office, and the computing department of the Census Bureau.

Barry looked at him in open-eyed wonder. He had the usual amount of boyish enthusiasm upon the subject of sight-seeing, but he could not understand the motive that would lead a man to visit what he considered the dullest departments of the Government.

"What in the world did you visit the Census Bureau for?" he asked.

"To satisfy the curiosity which I inherited from Mother Eve," was the dry response.

"But," protested Barry, "it is nothing but figures, and to me figures are so dry."

"Well, it is all a question of taste, my boy. To my mind there is nothing in the world so romantic and so fascinating as figures. I would sooner add up a column of figures any day in the week than read the finest poem that was ever written."

Barry shook his head.

"I can't understand that feeling," he said.

"I suppose not, but anyhow, this census business has a special attraction for me. I wondered how they computed the figures after they gathered them."

"Well, did you find out?"

"I did, indeed. If the boys at the Cleverly school want any information on this subject, all they have to do is to call on their 'Uncle Daniel.'"

In the midst of their conversation the voice of Mr. Carlton rang out warningly:

"Gentlemen, we haven't a minute to spare. The Committee will be called to order on the stroke of two, and we should be present. Just come with me."

He started away from the room and they followed him in single file. They marched through the subway which leads from the office building of the House of Representatives into the Capitol. In a few minutes they reached the headquarters of the Committee on Naval Affairs. The members were already in session. A quick survey of the room showed John Carlton that Mr. Jesse Hudson was in his place at the right hand of the Chairman of the Committee. Joel Phipps, the clerk of the Committee, for whom Mr. Carlton had no great relish, was calling the roll in a sing-song voice. Carlton wondered vaguely whether Hudson would openly oppose his bill, and if so, on what ground he would base his opposition. Hudson, on his part, gave no intimation of his intentions. He nodded curtly to Carlton on his entrance, and then buried himself in the perusal of a document that he held in his hand.

Presently the business before the Committee was taken up in regular order. Several of the members made motions for the purpose of regulating the method of considering the various bills that were about to be brought to their attention. Hudson was one of these. He reminded the Committee that it was their policy not to consider propositions from cities or towns having a population of less than thirty thousand. This, he said, was necessary because of the labor problem.

Mr. Carlton now arose and said that he desired to have the privilege of presenting arguments to prove that the city of Cleverly should have the new Naval Repair Station, and that he wished to introduce a number of his constituents who had visited Washington for that purpose. The first member who was introduced was Postmaster Ford, who was put forward as a man who was in a position to understand the Government side of the question.

Mr. Ford made an effective little speech, in which he presented statistics to show that Cleverly was just the place for the station. He said that the increasing importance of the place justified the people in making this request. When one of the members suggested that the proposed site might be far from the ocean, he said that very thing insured the Government a fresh-water basin where the barnacles could be readily cleaned from the largest battleships afloat.

Mr. Smithers was then presented to the Committee, and the force and originality of his remarks immediately attracted the attention of the members. He had the valuable faculty of saying commonplace things in a very impressive manner, and he proved to be the best speaker of the delegation. He dwelt upon the growth of Cleverly, and said that it was the duty of the National Government, not only to keep step with local progress, but, if possible, always to be a few paces in advance.

After Mr. Smithers had taken his seat, the President of the local Board of Trade told the members that the growing importance of Cleverly as a business centre justified the demand which the citizens were making upon the Congress of the United States. The members of the Committee were beginning to get a little bit bored by this time, and they did not pay much attention to the array of facts which the speaker presented in support of his contentions.

As he sat down Mr. Carlton arose, and turning to the members, said:

"Gentlemen, have you any questions to ask of my constituents? If so, I know that they will be only too glad to answer them."

The members shook their heads, as much as to say that they had heard as much as they cared to hear, but this did not satisfy Mr. Carlton. He desired, if possible, to spike any opposition that might develop. He turned and looked directly at Jesse Hudson.

"Mr. Hudson, have you any questions to ask?"

"No," said Hudson, in a slow-going way, "I've listened to all that has been said, and I have no desire to combat any of the arguments which have been presented."

Carlton beamed with delight. He had no idea that his proposition would have such plain sailing. He turned to the head of the Committee and said:

"I suppose, Mr. Chairman, that it would not be premature if I were to tell the members of this Committee that the proposition for a new Naval Repair Station for Cleverly is likely to be reported to Congress with a favorable report?"

"I think that what you say is quite probable," said the Chairman. "For my own part I—"

"One moment," interrupted a determined voice.

Every eye was turned in that direction and discovered Jesse Hudson on his feet, gazing at Carlton in a menacing manner.

"Mr. Hudson has the floor," said the Chairman, respectfully.

"Now, gentlemen," said Hudson, in his bristling, aggressive way, "before we go any further in the business that is before this Committee, I move that we throw out the proposition to give this station to Cleverly."

"Why?" demanded Carlton. "I think we have made it a good case."

"You have made it a splendid case," was the sneering response, "but unfortunately Cleverly is a city that does not come within the scope of the work which has been mapped out by this Committee."

"What do you mean?" demanded Carlton, angrily.

"I mean that we agreed that we should not consider the application of cities or towns with a population of less than thirty thousand."

"I know that," assented Carlton, "but—"

"There are no 'buts' to it," cried the other, exultingly. "I have here an official copy of the last census," and he held a document in the air, "and according to this book, Cleverly has a population of 29,786."

Carlton looked crestfallen. The other members of the Committee yawned. One of them said with a snicker:

"We have wasted a lot of valuable time."

"Yes," remarked another, "I move that we take up the next bill before the Committee."

"But," protested Carlton, "the figures Mr. Hudson has given are eight or nine years old."

"Yes," retorted his adversary, "but they are the only official figures we can consider."

"One moment," cried a voice from the rear of the room.

Everybody looked in that direction. Mr. Daniel Smithers was standing up and waving a sheet of paper in the air.

"This gentleman is not a member of the Committee," protested Hudson.

"No," shouted the schoolmaster, "but I have some information that the Committee might like to receive."

"What is it?" asked the Chairman.

"It is simply this: I was in the office of the Director of the Census less than an hour ago. He was good enough to tell me that the computers had just finished the count of the new census of the city of Cleverly."

"Yes, yes," cried Carlton, on his feet, "and what were the figures? What is the population of Cleverly today?"

Smithers straightened to his full height in order to fire his shot straight at the bull's eye. He spoke impressively, even dramatically:

"Cleverly, today," he cried, "has a population of 43,986!"

Two or three members of the Committee and the entire delegation from Cleverly broke out in a ripple of applause. Hudson, seated in a corner of the room, looked sick and crestfallen. The Chairman of the Committee turned to the clerk and said, drily:

"Lay the Cleverly bill aside. It is evidently worthy of further consideration."

The Chairman of the delegation thanked the members of the Committee for their attention and then filed out of the room, with Carlton at their head. As they reached the corridor of the Capitol, the big statesman grabbed the schoolteacher by the hand and cried, impulsively:

"By George, Smithers, but you just came in in the very nick of time!"

Smithers smiled in his homely way.

"I guess it was all right," he admitted, "but, John, don't you remember when we were boys, they used to say I was the best pinch hitter on our base-ball team?"

CHAPTER XIII
A LITTLE PILGRIMAGE

That night Congressman Carlton entertained the Cleverly delegation at dinner. It was a merry party, for they all felt very happy over their preliminary victory in the matter of the new Federal station. Barry was included among the dinner guests, and he conducted himself with due modesty, and yet with all of the confidence of a veteran statesman. The episode of the afternoon naturally came in for a large share of conversation. The various members of the party viewed it according to their respective methods of viewing life.

"I think we might as well go ahead and advertise for proposals," said Postmaster Ford, who had the reputation of being the most optimistic man in Cleverly. "The bill's as good as passed. It's a sure thing!"

Congressman Carlton laughed.

"I wish you would loan me your rose-colored glasses, Ford," was his comment; "you certainly look on the sunny side of things."

"It's the only way to succeed," was the jovial response. "I think pessimists should be suppressed by law."

"What do you think of that, Mr. Blake?" asked the legislator, turning to Barry's uncle.

Hiram was a cautious man. He paused for some moments before replying. He spoke, finally, with great deliberation:

"I think it's a great mistake for any of us, either as individuals or as a community, to count our chickens before they are hatched."

Daniel Smithers had remained silent during the interchange of views. John Carlton glanced in his direction.

"What has the philosopher of Cleverly to say on the burning subject of the hour?"

The schoolmaster modestly disclaimed the title, saying that as far as wisdom was concerned, there was safety in numbers.

"But what do you think of the situation?" insisted the Congressman.

"Well," said the other, "I think Ford and Blake are extremists. I see no occasion for either joy or sorrow."

"Smithers is hedging," called a voice from the other side of the table.

"Not at all," protested the teacher. "As I view the situation, we have every reason to be satisfied. We have won the skirmish, but the big battle is still to be fought. Moreover, it does not take a very bright observer to see that Mr. Carlton has a very resourceful and determined adversary in Jesse Hudson. He was very much chagrined over his setback this afternoon, and if I am not very much mistaken in my man he will do his best to keep Cleverly from getting the new Naval Repair Station."

Mr. Carlton nodded his head.

"You've sized the situation up to the dot. There's no use blinking our eyes to the truth. I'm up against the hardest fight of my life. While you're with me, gentlemen, I feel your enthusiasm and strength. But when you go away you must not forget that—"

"That you'll be standing all alone against a combination of clever politicians," interrupted Hiram Blake.

The Congressman laughed.

"That's not exactly what I intended to say," he remarked, "but we'll let it go at that."

"Blake's wrong in one particular," observed Smithers.

"How?"

"You won't be alone in this fight."

"No?"

"No; you'll have Barry Wynn with you."

Barry, sitting at the far end of the table, blushed to the roots of his hair.

In the evening the delegation went to one of the theatres in Washington as the guests of John Carlton. He purchased an entire box in honor of the occasion, and thus his friends were able to see and hear to great advantage. The play was one of James M. Barrie's whimsical comedies, and to say that they all enjoyed it would be putting it very mildly indeed. The company was competent and the play itself was not only humorous but wholesome as well. Cleverly, while a thriving town, did not always have the privilege of seeing the best plays, and, as a consequence, this visit to the theatre in Washington was an opportunity that was remembered a long while by each member of the delegation.

After the performance Congressman Carlton escorted his friends to their hotel, and as they were about to part for the night, he said:

"Well, gentlemen, I shall be engaged all day tomorrow with my official duties, and I am going to place you in the hands of Barry Wynn. He will act as my representative. Now, is there anything in particular that you would like to do tomorrow?"

One after another said that they had no special object in view. Finally, Mr. Carlton turned to the boy and said:

"Barry, what do you say? What suggestion have you to make?"

Barry, thus suddenly appealed to, was at a loss what to say. In a moment or two, however, a thought flashed into his mind and he gave it voice:

"I think a trip to Mount Vernon would come pretty nearly filling the bill."

"Good!" ejaculated the Congressman. "I can think of nothing that would be pleasanter or more profitable. A pilgrimage to the tomb of Washington! It's the very thing."

Everybody agreed to the proposition and a call was left with the night clerk at the hotel so that they would be able to have an early breakfast and start out on their trip in good season. They had all breakfasted by nine o'clock the following morning and were ready for the day's sight seeing. The trip was made by rail, and after reaching the home of the Father of his Country, the members separated and spent nearly two hours in viewing every part of the historic estate. They were all enchanted with the simplicity of Mount Vernon. Standing on the colonial porch, they could look out and see the Potomac river shimmering in the distance. Mr. Smithers voiced the general opinion when he said that Washington could not have secured a more ideal residence in which to spend his honorable old age.

Although they were all men, the members of the delegation were greatly interested in the quaint dining-room, and they admired the Colonial china, the antique furniture, and the picturesque surroundings. They stood in the hallway and looked up the open staircase, which Nellie Custis had walked down one beautiful morning to become a bride. Indeed, they were all intelligent men, and all having read the life of Washington and the history of the country to advantage, they associated every part of the old mansion with some interesting anecdote.

Mr. Smithers was particularly interested in the boyish recollections of the great Washington. He gazed with particular keenness on the little bundle of books which the future President of the country had read with such profit when a boy. He examined minutely the fragments of school exercises which showed the round, fair handwriting which has since become so familiar to the civilized world. He noted among the papers many copies of legal forms written by the youthful Washington, as well as the set of rules regarding behavior. It was evident that these rules, while sounding somewhat stilted, had had a remarkable effect in moulding the boy's mind and in forming his character.

"Look at this one, Barry," said the old schoolmaster, "it is worth remembering."

Barry looked over the shoulder of his old friend and read:

> "Labor to keep alive in your breast that little spark of celestial fire called 'conscience.'"

Hiram Blake and Postmaster Ford, who were standing back of the other two, nodded their assent and indicated by their manner, if not in words, that a boy who would keep that maxim before him at all times could not fail to become a useful member of society.

"Here's another one worth hearing," called out Mr. Smithers.

"What is it?" asked Hiram.

"Let your discourse with men of business be short and comprehensive,"

read the schoolmaster, slowly.

"Good," cried Postmaster Ford. "That should be printed on a card and placed on the desk of every busy man. It might frighten off the bores."

All the members of the party were now straining to see the little book, which was kept out of the reach of vandals. Hiram Blake read a maxim as follows:

"Speak not evil of the absent, for it is unjust."

The Postmaster recited the next one:

"Undertake not what you cannot perform, but be careful to keep your promise."

Before they left, the attendant of the estate gave them an outline of the history of Mount Vernon. He said that it was the property of the Mount Vernon Association, which had incorporated many years before for the purpose of purchasing and holding the estate in perpetuity. The association, he added, was composed of ladies of the United States and was ably managed by a Board of lady Regents. Mount Vernon descended to George Washington when he was about twenty-one years of age, from his half brother, Lawrence Washington, and from that time until his death, on the 14th of December, 1799, it was his home.

The time had passed so quickly and so pleasantly that it was now almost noon, and it was decided that if they desired to reach their hotel in time for lunch, they would have to move at once. As they were about to pass out of the grounds, a large automobile came round one corner of the property, prepared to resume its journey to the Capitol. Four gentlemen were in this party. They had been inspecting Mount Vernon at the same time as the delegation from Cleverly. The gentleman in charge, who appeared to be paying a great deal of attention to the other three, was rather dignified. But he had a very agreeable manner and frequently said things that caused his companions to laugh.

Barry had been watching this gentleman for some time, and now he stood gazing at him as though he were fascinated. There was something familiar about him. Barry felt that he had met him before and yet, try as he could, the memory of such a meeting would not come to his mind.

While Barry was still engaged in this mental debate, a sudden gust of wind came along and took the stranger's hat from his head. It fell to the ground and being lifted up again by the breeze, started off toward the Potomac river, with the certainty and speed of a bird. Barry did not hesitate, not even for a fraction of a second. He started after the truant hat as fast as his legs would carry him.

It was a wild chase, but the boy won. He picked up the head-piece and started back breathless but triumphant. The gentleman came running toward him, meet-

A LITTLE PILGRIMAGE 67

ing him half way. The incident had not disturbed his temper. He was in the best of good humor.

"You're a better sprinter than I," he said, jovially, "but when I was your age I think I could have beaten you."

The boy and the man stood talking for some moments. The gentleman was evidently asking many questions and Barry, very much embarrassed, was answering the best he could.

"Looks as if Barry had made a new friend," commented Mr. Smithers.

Before anyone had a chance to reply, Barry was escorting the stranger towards the delegation from Cleverly. He presented each of them in their turn, but he was so flustered that no one caught the name of the newcomer. Mr. Smithers and Postmaster Ford, however, looked at the stranger very curiously and there was something very much like reverence in their eyes. He chatted very amiably for a few moments and spoke about the historic importance of the ground on which they were standing.

"By the by," he said, turning to Barry, "you're a page boy; do you know Mr. John Carlton?"

"He's the member that had me appointed," replied Barry, proudly.

"Good," was the cordial response, "I'm glad to hear it. Carlton is an able man and," half musingly, "he's a coming man, too; a coming man."

The members of the delegation looked at one another significantly. It was a pleasure to them to hear anyone commend their Congressman. Presently the stranger prepared to depart.

"I am very glad to have seen you gentlemen here," he said. "I think that every man who has the opportunity to pay a pilgrimage to Mount Vernon should do so."

They agreed with him, and presently, after some more talk, he turned and said:

"Where's that little page boy?"

Barry was pushed to the front, and the stranger shook hands with him very cordially.

"It does me good to shake hands with you," he said. "I like all boys, but I have a special liking for boys who are bright and ambitious."

The next moment he had stepped into the automobile with his friends, and as the machine puffed out of the gateway, he turned in his seat and waved his hand, exclaiming:

"Good-bye, and good luck to you all."

It was all done so quickly that the visitors scarcely had time to get their bearings. Hiram Blake, who had been looking after the vanishing machine like a man in a stupor, was the first to speak:

"Who is that man?" he demanded.

"That," answered Barry, proudly, "is the President of the United States!"

"I thought so," commented Mr. Smithers; "he had the air of a man of authority."

"Yes," remarked Postmaster Ford, "I was sure it was he, and he looks just like his pictures."

An hour later the members were taking their lunch at the hotel in Washington, and before dusk that evening, they had started on their return trip to Cleverly.

"Good-bye," cried Congressman Carlton, who was on the station platform as they boarded the train, "I will promise to do the best I can with that bill."

Mr. Smithers, who was the last one to get on the train, thought of the incident at Mount Vernon, and replied significantly:

"I am sure you won't fail us—not when you have the assistance of such a bright boy as Barry Wynn."

CHAPTER XIV
BARRY FALLS A SECOND TIME

For several days after his unexpected interview with the President, Barry was filled with a sense of his own importance. He related the incident to Congressman Carlton and to Joe Hart, and in the course of time, it became very generally known about the Capitol. Mr. Carlton seemed very much pleased at the honor that had been shown to his protégé, but the page boys received the story in silence. Barry attributed their attitude to envy, and that fact caused him to walk about with his chin very high in the air. Indeed, he felt like a boy who was walking on clouds. To use the words of one of the messengers at the Capitol, he "didn't know whether he stood on his head or his heels."

A great deal of praise had been accorded him at the time of the Warrington incident, and he was pointed out as the page boy who had been instrumental in saving an important piece of legislation in which the President was personally interested. The visit of the delegation from Cleverly also caused him much self-gratification. The words of Mr. Smithers to Congressman Carlton were still ringing in his ears. He could hear the old teacher yet as he called out to the Congressman:

"I am sure you won't fail us—not when you have the assistance of such a bright boy as Barry Wynn."

All of these things combined had the effect of making him feel that the fate of a nation—in a measure—depended upon him. He even became somewhat frigid in his relations with Joe Hart.

Barry, without knowing it, was passing through that period which comes to nearly every boy,—the period between boyhood and manhood, when self-importance is apt to overshadow and conceal real worth. But, whatever the cause, there was no doubt of the effect that he produced. He succeeded effectively in winning the ill will of the other boys. They naturally resented the idea of a new page receiving so much praise from the members of Congress.

The Sergeant-at-Arms of the House had provided the boys with a dressing room in one of the alcoves in the basement of the Capitol, and they frequently assembled here when not otherwise engaged. It was provided with basins, towels, clothes-closets, and the other furnishings of a room of this character. On cloudy days it was quite dark in this apartment. On the third day after the Presidential adventure, Barry hurried down to this room to wash his hands and comb his hair before beginning his duties at the noonday session of the House. It was a gloomy day, but he managed to find his way to the wash-basin. He opened the spigot and filled the receptacle with water. At that moment one of the boys attracted his attention to something that was going on in another part of the room, and in the interval another little fellow crept over to the basin and poured something into the water. Barry, all unsuspecting of what had gone on in the brief interval, returned to the basin and hastily washed his face and hands and then, boy-like, gave his hair a quick smooth-down with a brush that lay on the marble wash table.

"Barry! Barry!" cried a voice at the door. "Mr. Carlton wants you right away."

"I will come in a minute," was the reply. "I want to see if my hair's all right."

"You haven't any time for that," was the retort. "He's calling you, and he'll be very angry if you don't come at once."

Without further ado, Barry hurried up the marble stairway and along the corridor and into the House. Several persons who passed him on the way, looked at him and laughed, but he paid no attention to them. Presently he reached the House and hurried over to where Mr. Carlton sat. The Congressman looked at him for a moment and then burst into laughter.

"Why, Barry," he exclaimed, "what in the world is the matter with you?"

"Nothing," said the boy, innocently. "I was told that you wanted me in a hurry."

"No," was the answer, "I don't want you, but if I were you I'd go and wash my face before I began my duties."

"Wash my face?" echoed Barry. "What do you mean?"

"Why, you look as though you had just emerged from darkest Africa."

Wonderingly, Barry left the House and went out into the corridor again. He went down stairs and before going back into the dressing room, took a look at himself in a big pier mirror. What he saw caused him to gasp with horror. His face was all black and smeared. He looked at his hands. They were no better. As he turned from the glass a roar of laughter greeted him. A crowd of the boys stood behind him, giggling and going through all sorts of contortions. Barry turned from the glass indignantly. As he started into the dressing room he saw Joe Hart.

"What does this mean," he exclaimed.

"It means that the boys have given you the first degree."

And such proved to be the case. A mischievous page boy had deliberately emptied a bottle of ink in the wash basin with a consequence that had been fatal to Barry's dignity. He did not take it in good part. Indeed, he threatened to thrash the boy who had been guilty of the offense. At this exhibition of temper the boys all filed down stairs after him, and when they were safely away from public view, surrounded the new page and told him to take his place on an elevated platform. He gazed at them defiantly, but fight was out of the question. There were at least ten boys in the crowd, and he realized that at the first move he made they were likely to pounce on him and possibly tear the clothes from his back. So he determined to submit with the best grace possible.

BARRY FALLS A SECOND TIME

"Now," said one tall fellow, who appeared to be the ringleader, "we want you to recite your lesson."

"My lesson?"

"Yes," said the other, handing him a large volume, "your lesson, and if you don't do it correctly you'll be kept in after school."

Barry took the big book obediently. It was an unabridged dictionary.

"Now," said the moving spirit, "turn to the letter E."

Barry did so.

"Please find the word 'egotism.'"

Barry obeyed.

"Have you got it?"

"Yes," said Barry.

"Well, read the definition of the word as you find it in that book."

Barry did as he was bid, just as a pupil would respond to the commands of his teacher.

"Egotism," he read, "is the practice of too frequently using the word 'I'; hence a speaking or writing overmuch of one's self; self-exaltation; self-praise; the act or practice of magnifying one's self or parading one's doings."

"Correct," cried the chief of the bad boys. "You're likely to be promoted. You may report for duty to the Sergeant-at-Arms."

It is hardly necessary to say that Barry did not relish this ceremony. Mr. Carlton, when he learned of the affair a day or so later, laughed. He wondered if, after all, Barry did not need the punishment. However, whatever the feelings of those most concerned, it had a chastening effect on the new page boy. But it did not entirely deprive him of his feeling of self-importance, and he continued to keep most of his fellow pages at a distance.

It was about this time that Barry began to realize that, even with his youth and inexperience, he was likely to be in the midst of great happenings. There had been a "lagging" tendency in Congress. The President had been urging important legislation from the very beginning of the session, but a strong opposition effectively blocked him. The big party leaders, it must be confessed, were not entirely in sympathy with the chief executive of the nation, and as a consequence, their support of his pet measures was lukewarm and lacking in the effectiveness which produces successful legislation. Jesse Hudson was counted among the President's supporters, although his actions did not give color to the assumption; John Carlton, on the other hand, was classed among the neutral members of the House, but was outspoken in the advocacy of certain bills which the President had at heart.

There was something about the very air of Washington that portended a political storm. The House seemed to be "marking time," as far as the business of the nation was concerned. The President, in the White House at the other end of the long avenue, was plainly dissatisfied with the condition of affairs. Few expressed their convictions publicly, but every now and then hints were dropped which suggested the possibility of a big political contest. Those who loved war for the sake of the fighting, begged Carlton to throw down the gage of battle, but he smiled that wise smile of his—and said nothing.

During all of this time a sort of armed neutrality existed between John Carlton and Jesse Hudson. On the morning after the day that Barry had his experience with his fellow pages, Mr. Carlton got into a controversy with Congressman Hudson on the floor of the House. It began in a debate over a certain clause in the tariff bill. Hudson made an assertion which was combated by Carlton. For a few moments there was a running fire of assertions and contradictions. Finally Hudson challenged Carlton for proof of the statements which he made.

"Mr. Speaker," said the latter, "if the gentleman from Illinois will indulge me, I think I can produce the proof of my assertion before the conclusion of this debate. It will be necessary, however, for me to procure a certain book which is now in the Congressional Library."

Hudson arose with a mocking smile.

"I will give the gentleman all the time he desires, and all the rope he wants, because I feel satisfied that if I give him enough he will eventually hang himself."

The members of the House laughed at this retort, and then proceeded with the consideration of the bills before them. Mr. Carlton clapped his hands and Barry rushed to his side.

"Barry," he said, "I want you to hurry over to the Congressional Library and get me a copy of a book which contains a report showing the wages paid to certain workmen of Birmingham, England."

To make certain that he would obtain exactly what he wanted, the Congressman gave Barry a memorandum containing the name of the volume desired. Ordinarily, when a member desires to obtain a book from the Library of Congress, he utilizes a device for transporting books between the library and the Capitol. It is a pneumatic tube running from the library to a small receiving room just back of Statuary Hall. Books, as a rule, are obtained very expeditiously in this manner, but Mr. Carlton was so anxious that there should be no error that he decided to send Barry personally to the Librarian of Congress.

The boy hurried on his errand and in a few minutes was in the library. He presented the memorandum to the official in charge, and in a few minutes had obtained the book that was desired. While he was waiting, he gazed about the building with wondering eyes. It was the first visit that he had made to this beautiful structure, and he readily believed the assertion of one of the attendants that it was the handsomest building for public purposes in the world. After he had obtained the book for Mr. Carlton, he walked through the labyrinth of beauty, gazing with wide-open eyes on the treasures of art and sculpture that met him at every turn. Imaginary figures of History, Science, and Art stood out at every point in the long corridors and galleries. It was so well lighted and ventilated that the boy felt that he was in a bookish Paradise.

After going through the galleries he finally went into the library proper and gazed at many of the curiosities of literature that abounded in that place. He was examining a copy of Eliot's Indian Bible, published in Cambridge in 1669, when the striking of a clock aroused him to a realization of the business that had brought him to the library. He remembered, with a pang of remorse, that Mr. Carlton was probably still waiting for the book that he had under his arm.

He hastened back to the House. As he entered through one of the swinging doors he noticed that Jesse Hudson was on his feet.

"Now," he was saying, "if the gentleman from Maine is ready to produce the proof of the assertion that he made earlier in the day, I would like to have it."

Carlton arose from his seat in an apologetic manner.

"I am sorry to say that I have not yet secured the data I wanted."

Hudson, who was still standing, sneered at his adversary:

"Probably," he said, "it is because there is no such data!"

"Gentlemen, you will please refrain from indulging in personalities," warned the Speaker. "The question before the House is on the motion of the gentleman from Illinois. All in favor will please say 'Aye.'"

A roar of "Ayes" came from the members of the House.

The echo had scarcely died out when a voice from the corner could be heard:

"I move that the House do now adjourn."

"The members have heard the motion," said the Speaker. "All in favor of adjournment will please say 'Aye.'"

There was a roar of "Ayes."

"All who are opposed will say 'Nay.'"

A few scattered voices, among them Mr. Carlton's, cried "Nay."

"The 'Ayes' have it," declared the Speaker, "and the House now stands adjourned."

At that moment Barry reached Mr. Carlton's side, holding a copy of the much needed book in his hand. The Congressman turned around and the moment he saw the boy a glint of anger appeared in his eyes. John Carlton was a very amiable man, but like most men of that type, he could be exceedingly angry at times. The thought of the manner in which he had been worsted by his adversary did not help his temper at this particular moment. He waved his hand toward Barry with a motion of disgust:

"You may take the book back now," he said; "I have no use for it!"

"I am sorry, Mr. Carlton," began Barry, "but—"

"Your sorrow comes too late," was the angry retort, "I have done my best for you, and now you have succeeded in doing your worst for me!"

"But, Mr. Carlton—"

"I don't care for any explanation; I have nothing more to say."

And, turning on his heel, the Congressman walked away, leaving Barry standing in the aisle, flushed and embarrassed.

It was a very sore trial for the boy from Cleverly. When Barry sought his bed that night all of the vanity that had influenced his words and actions during the previous days had vanished. He realized that he had been at fault, and he wondered vaguely whether Mr. Carlton would ever forgive him for his carelessness. He tried to keep up bravely, but his pillow was damp with the tears that persisted in welling up in his eyes. He realized that, after all, he was only a boy, with all of the defects of boyhood. He thought of the lost money at the moving picture show, and then of the manner in which he had failed his benefactor at a very critical moment. After all, he was very, very human—and he had fallen a second time.

CHAPTER XV
BARRY REDEEMS HIMSELF

For many days after the unfortunate incident of the Congressional Library Barry found it very embarrassing to be in the presence of Mr. Carlton. He realized more deeply as time went on how greatly he had neglected his duty, and that fact did not tend to keep him in a very pleasant state of mind. He was morose, irritable, and dissatisfied with himself and with the world in general.

He still retained enough false pride to prevent him from making any overtures to his friend and benefactor. Besides that, he had come to know Mr. Carlton's character well enough to appreciate that soft words could not, with him, take the place of a plain performance of duty. Mr. Carlton, on his part, made no further reference to the incident. He did not treat Barry unkindly, but there was in his manner an absence of that cordiality that had existed before Barry's fall from grace.

To put it plainly, the friendly relations that had existed between the man and the boy, while not absolutely broken, were strained in a manner that made it very painful to Barry. He wondered in a heartsick way whether he would ever again be the same to his old friend. He dwelt upon the existing conditions all the time, and this only served to make him still more uncomfortable.

A few nights after the occurrence he made up his mind to write to his mother and make a frank confession of the whole business. He felt that it was due her and that it would be wrong for him to keep her in the dark. Almost immediately he received an impulsive, motherly reply. She said that she was very greatly chagrined to hear of the incident, but that she felt certain that it would be a warning to prevent him from failing in his duty in the future. She concluded by speaking of the great kindness of heart of John Carlton, and offered to write to him in behalf of her son. Barry was startled at this unexpected suggestion, and he lost no time in dispatching a reply in which he begged her very fervently not to think of writing to the Congressman. He said that he would have to depend on his own resources, and that under all circumstances he was willing to let events take their course.

During this trying period in his Washington career Barry had one good, loyal friend who never failed him. It is needless to say that this person was little Joe Hart. He was like a faithful dog that never deserts even in the days of greatest danger and trouble. He never obtruded his friendship on Barry, but he always managed to be by his side in his big-hearted way, snuggling up to the other in that half-whimsical, half-affectionate way which wholly won the heart of the boy from Cleverly. Joe was apologetic, explanatory, and defiant by turns.

"You're not the first fellow that ever made a slip," he said. "Why don't you go to Mr. Carlton and have it out with him?"

Barry smiled sadly.

"There is nothing to have 'out,' as you put it. Mr. Carlton says nothing. He won't even scold me, and for that reason it is impossible for me to explain or to talk back."

"Well," said Joe, reflectively, as he wiped his freckled face with the back of his hand, "then the only thing to do is to defy him."

"Defy him?" echoed Barry, in amazement.

"Yes, just tell him you're going to chuck up your job."

"Chuck up my job?" gasped Barry. "Why, I couldn't do that. I couldn't think of such a thing. I wouldn't dare go back to mother and tell her that I failed in Washington!"

"But," persisted the young diplomat, "Congress isn't the only thing in Washington. You can get a job as a telegraph boy, or you might become an office boy with one of the morning newspapers."

"I don't think I'd like that."

"Why, it's great," said Joe. "Felix Conway is right in with those people and he could get you on one of the papers. I know boys that started as messengers and afterwards became reporters."

Barry shook his head decidedly.

"I have no intention of resigning my position as page, and I don't think that Mr. Carlton desires it either."

"Very well," was the reply, with a resigned air. "If your mind's settled, I'm not going to try to change it."

"It's settled," said Barry.

"By the way," said Joe, changing the subject, "did you know that I had a typewriter?"

"No, I did not."

"Well, if you'll come up to my room, I'll show it to you. It's a second-hand affair. I bought it for fifteen dollars, but it has been fixed up so that it is almost as good as new. I have been learning to work it, and I think it might come in useful some day."

Barry was interested at once, and after supper that night he went up to Joe's room and examined the wonderful purchase of the page boy. Joe had not misrepresented the case at all. The machine was in fairly good repair. Joe sat down for the edification of his friend and wrote him a letter. It was a slow and somewhat painful process. He used one finger like a boarding-school miss who had not yet received her first lesson on the piano. Sometimes he struck a comma for a period, and occasionally he used a dash instead of an interrogation point, and when the letter

BARRY REDEEMS HIMSELF

was finished an unbiased observer would have immediately ranked it among the curiosities of literature. But it served its purpose, for it awoke a half-slumbering desire that Barry had in his mind ever since he came to Washington.

"Joe," he said, "I wonder if I couldn't go to one of those night schools and increase my speed in typewriting and stenography."

"Sure you could," was the reply; "I know a good place, and I'll take you there tonight if you want me to do it."

Barry was willing, and the two boys proceeded to one of the business colleges in the lower section of the city and obtained an interview with the manager. Barry placed his case very clearly.

"I am anxious to get speed in stenography and typewriting, and learn bookkeeping," he said, "and if I thought I could get through in three months I'd be glad to undertake it."

The teacher, thus appealed to, reflected a moment before replying, and then said:

"It all depends on your own ability. Some boys are quicker than others. If you want to join this school we will do the best we can for you within the time appointed. We have branches in all of the large cities, and if you do not get through here while you are in Washington you could readily finish your course elsewhere."

The terms were satisfactory, and Barry made his arrangements then and there. Indeed, he was so filled with the idea of perfecting himself that he started in to work that very night. Every evening thereafter, as soon as he had finished his supper, he went to the business college and for two or three hours was busy learning the intricacies of stenography and typewriting. Bookkeeping he finally decided to omit, feeling that he could make greater progress if he confined himself to the other two branches.

Three weeks had gone by and Barry was returning from his school one night when something prompted him to go into the office building of the members of Congress. He walked through the corridor leading to Mr. Carlton's office and noticed that a light was burning there. After a minute's hesitancy, he opened the door and walked in. Congressman Carlton was at his desk with a pile of papers about him. He greeted Barry very kindly:

"Hello!" he said; "glad to see you."

"Is there anything I can do?" asked Barry, as he gradually plucked up courage.

Mr. Carlton groaned and then made a grimace.

"I wish you could do something," he replied; "I've got 225 agricultural reports that ought to go out the first thing in the morning. Each one of them should be accompanied by a typewritten letter signed by myself. I have the books here, and a form of letter, but I haven't anybody to do the work. I've got to go to a Committee meeting in fifteen minutes and I am almost distracted."

"I think I might be able to help you out some," said the boy, timidly.

"Help me out?" said the Congressman, looking up in surprise.

"Yes," said Barry, "you know I work the typewriter, and I could easily copy your letters."

Mr. Carlton laughed in the joyous, care-free way that Barry remembered so well.

"Barry, you are very kind, but I don't think you could possibly get through with the work. I remember well when you wrote the bill for the Naval Repair Station. While you did it all right, you were certainly slower than the hearse at the colored funeral."

"Well," said Barry, becoming more confident as he talked, "if you will just let me go ahead I might finish some of the letters tonight, and you know every little helps."

Mr. Carlton meditated for a moment.

"Yes," he agreed, "that's true, but how about the agricultural reports? They would have to be addressed too."

"I have a friend who might help me out with that," suggested Barry.

"All right," said the Congressman, finally, "you may go ahead and do the best you can. Even if you only finish a few of the letters and we get off a part of the books, I will feel somewhat relieved."

Mr. Carlton left the room a few moments afterwards in order to attend the Committee meeting. He said that he would not be back that night, but would meet Barry early in the morning. Within fifteen minutes the young page had communicated with Joe Hart, and in less than a half hour's time that mischievous boy was engaged in the task of addressing the wrappers on the agricultural reports. Barry, in the meantime, had the list of addresses propped up in front of him and was hard at work on the typewriter in copying the form of letter which had been left there by Mr. Carlton. He was surprised at his own speed and accuracy. He went with some deliberation at first, but after that he "struck his gait," as they say in horse-race parlance, and before very long he was turning letters out at an astonishing rate of speed. For hour after hour the click of the typewriter could be heard in the empty office building, and finally, when the clock struck midnight every one of the letters had been finished and every one of the books had been properly addressed.

Barry and Joe started home, two very tired but very happy boys. Barry thought his fellow page deserved some return for his labor. He was at a loss as to just how he could repay him for the emergency work he had done so well. Presently, in a sly sort of way, he offered him a two-dollar note. Joe drew back.

"What's that for?" he asked.

"Simply a small return for what you've done tonight."

The little fellow drew himself up to his full height.

"That's an insult to my dignity," he said, proudly.

"I didn't mean to do that," said Barry, half abashed, "but I'd like you to know that I appreciate what you've done."

"You can't do that with money," said the other, with all of the assurance of a millionaire.

"How can I do it?"

"By not speaking of it," said the youngster, sharply.

Barry looked at him smilingly.

"You're a funny fellow, Joe," he said, finally.

"Oh," said the page, with a shrug of his shoulders, "I'm like the great corporation lawyers. I never do things by halves. It's either a whopping big fee or nothing at all."

They reached home in a few minutes. They both went to bed immediately and slept the sweet, refreshing sleep that comes to those who labor and who go to bed with a clear conscience.

The first thing in the morning Barry stopped in at the office building to see if the letters had been dispatched. Mr. Carlton was seated at his desk and he clapped his hands with satisfaction as he saw Barry peeping in the doorway.

"Come in, my boy," he said, "come in."

"I just wondered whether you had signed your letters," said the boy.

"Yes," replied the Congressman, in his old, jovial way. "They're all signed, sealed and delivered. Every blessed one of them has been mailed and so are the books, and it is a mighty big relief to me, I can assure you."

Barry stood there in an awkward, embarrassed sort of way. He looked at Mr. Carlton appealingly, but said nothing. The big Congressman arose from his chair, walked around to where the boy stood, and putting his arm around his shoulder, said:

"Yes, I know. I know just what you are thinking about, and I'll answer your unspoken question. It's all right, Barry, you have redeemed yourself."

CHAPTER XVI
A CALL OF THE HOUSE

On the morning after Barry's restoration to the favor of his old friend, John Carlton received an invitation to call at the White House. It was a supreme moment. The big Congressman, with all of his natural modesty, was not insensible of the honor that had been done him. It was half-expected and yet, paradoxical as it may seem, it was a surprise. He felt instinctively that he was to be consulted on the political and legislative situation.

Republics differ from monarchies in many ways. The President is not a king, and yet a request from him is regarded as a command. It is no mean honor to be the confidant and adviser of the chief of a great nation, and Carlton, realizing this, lost no time in going to the White House.

The news that the Congressman was closeted with the President spread through Washington like a prairie fire after an August drought. It came, if the metaphor may be changed, like a crash of thunder after a long, sultry day. Already the political atmosphere was clearing. Many members, who had been on both sides of great questions, were preparing to scamper to cover. Men who had been on the fence, so to speak, were now making ready to drop down on either side. They knew that the talk between the Congressman and the President would mean a realignment of forces. The interview lasted for a long while, and after it was over Carlton came out of the White House with a look of determination on his strong face.

A few minutes after he returned, he called a conference of a few of his intimate friends and political associates in his private office. Barry Wynn, as a trusted page boy, acted as door tender and admitted only those who were known to be loyal adherents of the administration.

"Gentlemen," said Mr. Carlton, "I have had a long talk with the President and he is sincerely anxious to pass certain measures that have been introduced in the House at this session and which are intended to be for the benefit of the people. He feels that unless some radical steps be taken in this direction at once, he will be accused of insincerity, and he has asked me to call a number of his friends together and map out a programme for securing this reform legislation. The most important bill that is to be pushed forward is the one providing for the establishment of a Postal Savings Bank. I have explained the situation to you and if you have any comments or suggestions to make I shall be glad to hear from you."

This introduction on the part of Mr. Carlton was followed by a general discussion which was participated in by all of the dozen gentlemen who were present. The concensus of opinion was that none of the important measures would get through the House unless provision was made for additional sessions. It was resolved, therefore, that a number of night sessions should be held and all present pledged themselves to remain at their posts until they had accomplished substantial results. Carlton was unanimously selected as the leader of the Administration forces, and he, in turn, picked out Congressmen Bright, Harrison and Brown as his assistants, their duty being to round up all the members within reach and try to have every man respond to his name on the call of the roll.

The caucus called by Mr. Carlton had scarcely adjourned when the participants discovered that a meeting of the opposing forces was being held in another part of the Capitol. It is difficult to keep things of this character quiet, and before long it had leaked out that the opponents of the Postal bill had resolved to resist all efforts to enact the measure into law. It was learned also that Congressman Roland was to be the spokesman of the opposition and that he had selected Congressmen Wood, Hudson and Collins as his lieutenants. Thus the two armies, properly officered and marshaled, were ready for the coming fray.

The first night session was scheduled for the coming evening. All of the officers and employees of the House received instructions to be at their posts by eight o'clock sharp. Barry and Joe Hart left their boarding house nearly an hour before that time in order that they might report punctually to the Sergeant-at-Arms. As they walked along Pennsylvania Avenue they got the first glimpse of the dome of the Capitol illuminated by electricity. It was a brilliant sight. The night was dark and the lights seemed to dot the heavens without any support, shining out with all the glory of the stars themselves.

Within the Capitol the scene was no less brilliant and much more animated. The electric lights from the ceiling and the sides of the House made the great hall lighter than it was in midday. The Speaker sat in his usual place beneath the sheltering folds of the American flag. The galleries were crowded with an expectant audience, and when the presiding officer tapped his gavel on the marble desk a large percentage of the membership was seated.

After the usual routine preliminaries had been disposed of, John Carlton secured recognition and called up for consideration his Postal Savings bill, which was then on final consideration. An animated debate followed, and in the course of it, one of the opponents of the bill suddenly rose in his place and demanded a roll call, asserting that a quorum of the House was not present. In a few minutes everything was in confusion and the members and the Speaker threatened to be helplessly entangled in the intricate maze of parliamentary law. Out of it all, a few minutes later, came a call of the House.

Carlton and his lieutenants were on the alert at once. Their first care was to see that none of those present managed to escape from the room. It was quite late, and the enforced confinement began to have an irritating effect on the members. Some of them yawned and gaped as though the whole proceeding bored them more than words could express; others quarreled with their neighbors and threatened to do all sorts of unreasonable things if the doors were not thrown open; others, again, tried to reason with their colleagues and explain the necessity of the night sessions; a few of a philosophic frame of mind, composed themselves to the long siege that was before them. Several of them calmly stretched themselves on the sofas against the walls and peacefully proceeded to go to sleep. A few others, without much regard for the dignity of the House, put their heels on the desks and settled their heads on the backs of their chairs and dozed away their feeling of fatigue.

Carlton, who was here, there, and everywhere, had a hurried conference with his three lieutenants and laid his plans for the first stages of the big battle. It was midnight when the call of the House was ordered. The doors were closed and 127 members were found to be present. The House went into a Committee of the Whole, only to come out of it again, and the clerk called the roll again and again until his voice threatened to give way. The Speaker by this time had dispatched the Sergeant-at-Arms and his assistants to bring in the truant members.

At this stage of the game John Carlton very quietly utilized several of the page boys for the purpose of summoning members whom he knew would be only too glad to comply with his wishes. Barry Wynn was one of these and Joe Hart was another. Barry's list comprised four members whom Carlton knew would vote for the bill in which he was so deeply interested.

The first name on his list was Congressman Henry. Barry knew that this gentleman was living at the Cosmopolis Hotel and he proceeded there on a bicycle which he had borrowed for the occasion from a fellow page. The big hotel was deserted and the night clerk, seated in a chair behind the desk, was dreaming of pleasanter things than night sessions and unruly members. Barry awoke him instantly by demanding that he send his card to Congressman Henry.

The clerk wiped his eyes, gazed at the boy who stood before him, and then shook his head lazily.

"Nothing doing, young man," he said. "Mr. Henry is probably sound asleep and I don't propose to wake him up at this hour of the night."

"But, it's very urgent," insisted Barry. "There is a night session of Congress and there has been a call of the House."

"I don't care," was the reckless reply; "I would not call him for the President of the United States!"

"Where is his room?" asked Barry, with sudden inspiration flashing through his mind.

"His room is number 40 on the second floor."

"All right," said the boy, turning away and walking down the corridor.

Instead of going out of the hotel, however, he turned up the marble hallway and made his way to the second floor. The corridor was dimly lighted but he proceeded on his way until he came opposite room number 40. He looked twice to assure himself of the number and then pounded lustily on the door. A mumbling voice came from the bed-clothes:

"What do you want, anyhow?"

For reply Barry pounded harder than ever. There was a grumbling sound and presently the key was turned in the door, and a big man in pajamas came out. He glared at Barry fiercely.

"What do you want, to wake a man up at this hour of the night?"

"Why, Mr. Henry," said Barry, "I came to say—"

"Henry?" roared the other, with the voice of a mad bull. "My name isn't Henry!"

Barry's heart sank. He looked at the big person timidly and said:

"Why, aren't you Congressman Henry?"

"No," thundered the other, "I'm not Congressman Henry!"

"But, but—" stammered the boy, "I was told that Mr. Henry was in room 40."

Once again the man's voice roared through the length of the corridor:

"Room 40! You little blackguard, this is not room 40. This is room 4. Forty is at the other end of the corridor."

"I beg your pardon," stuttered the boy. "I didn't mean—"

"I don't care what you mean, or what you didn't mean," grumbled the man, "but I'd like to know what right you have to wake up people who are sound asleep. I'll complain to the clerk and find out what kind of a house this is, anyhow!"

Before he had finished the sentence, Barry was halfway down the corridor and finally reached the room he was looking for. He knocked on this door a little less defiantly than he had on the first one. In a little while it was opened, and the real Congressman stood there wanting to know why he had been aroused. Barry hastily explained his mission. Mr. Henry took it quite good-naturedly and said:

"All right, my boy, I will dress and get down to the Capitol in a few minutes."

From the Cosmopolis Barry went to another hotel a few blocks below, where he knew that Congressman Yale lived. To his delight he found this gentleman in the barber's chair indulging in the luxury of a shave. He knew Mr. Yale, and when that gentleman saw him he wanted to know his business. He told him in a few words and said that he would like to know if he was willing to hurry to the House.

"Willing," echoed the other; "I'm not very, but I'll go."

He did not wait for the barber to finish his shave, but told him that he need not go any further, and jumping out of the chair, he took a towel and wiped the lather from his face. Putting on his hat and coat, he hurried out of the hotel on to the avenue and thence towards the Capitol.

Jones, the third man on Barry's list, lived a few blocks away in a private house. The attendant who answered the door said that the Congressman had been to the theatre with his wife, but that he expected him almost any minute. While they were talking at the door Jones and his wife came up the steps, and when the law-maker found out the condition of affairs, he excused himself to his wife and promised Barry that he would report to John Carlton within the next fifteen minutes.

The last person that Barry was called upon to summon was Congressman Hutchinson. This gentleman was found in the library of his home, with his right foot wrapped in bandages, and propped up in a chair. He was not in a very good humor, and when Barry was ushered into his den he turned to him angrily and said:

"What in the world do you want with me?"

"Mr. Carlton wants you," said Barry, timidly. "There has been a call of the House and he wants you to come up as soon as you can and vote on the Postal Savings bill."

Mr. Hutchinson did not reply in words at once. He brought his fist with a bang on the table that stood next to the chair, and then he emphasized his disgust by picking up a book that lay on the table and throwing it at a cat that was sleeping in a corner of the room. After this strange and unexpected proceeding, a smile gradually crept over his stern countenance and he said:

"I feel a little better now, and I'll try to accommodate John."

"I know that he'll be glad," ventured Barry.

"Yes, I suppose he will," was the retort, "and I will be glad, too, if I can go over. I doubt if I can ever succeed in getting a shoe on this game foot of mine."

He summoned his servant and for the next fifteen minutes he was engaged in trying to put a shoe on his gouty foot. It was a painful proceeding, interspersed with remarks that would not look well in print, but presently the task was completed and in a little while afterwards Congressman Hutchinson was fully dressed and ready for his journey to the House.

A servant, in the meantime, had summoned a taxicab and the legislator took Barry in the machine with him. The dash to the Capitol was made in record-breaking time, and the clock was striking one as Barry entered the House with Mr. Hutchinson leaning on his arm. Their entrance was a signal for loud applause from both sides of the House.

In the meantime, during Barry's absence the Sergeant-at-Arms and his assistants had been doing their duties and one by one the captured absentees had stood up before the Speaker and tried to present some plausible reason for their failure to appear. Barry's willing captive was the last to come into the House.

"Mr. Hutchinson," said the Speaker, sternly, "you have absented yourself from the House during its sitting contrary to law and without the leave of the House. What excuse have you to offer?"

"The best excuse in the world," said the accused one, lifting his leg up very painfully. "My excuse is rheumatic gout."

A roar of laughter greeted this sally, and helped to restore the peevish mem-

A CALL OF THE HOUSE

bers to a condition approaching good humor.

After a final call of the roll, for the purpose of establishing a quorum, the debate was renewed and was carried on with much spirit for nearly an hour. At the end of that time Mr. Carlton demanded a roll call on the final passage of his Postal Savings bill. The leaders of the Opposition interposed various dilatory motions, but John Carlton swept them aside one by one. The strength and the power of his mind was never more firmly proven than on this historic occasion. He seemed to thrive on opposition. His strong brain seemed to grow keener and quicker as obstacles were placed in his way, but greatest of all, his iron will, no less than his great physical endurance, stood as a most effective barrier against repeated onslaughts of the minority.

The demand for the roll call was finally complied with, and each member answered to his name amid intense silence. The vote was pretty evenly divided, but when the last name had been called and it was shown that the bill had the number of votes required by law, a storm of applause broke out that lasted for several minutes.

It was almost daylight when the wearied members streamed out of the doors of the Capitol. John Carlton came along with a group of his admiring friends. He noticed Barry and Joe Hart and several other page boys standing near the doorway and called to them gaily:

"Boys, you all did well."

Barry and Joe walked home together that morning, and discussed the events of the night. Joe, looking at his friend in a furtive sort of way, said:

"Barry, do you remember that Mr. Carlton said we all did well?"

"Yes," said Barry, "I heard him say it and I was glad of it. I worked hard, but I didn't do a bit more than any of the other boys. I'm older now and more experienced than when I first came to Washington. I've got sense enough to realize that I'm only a little cog in a great big machine, and the work that I did was simply my duty and nothing more."

CHAPTER XVII
THE MISSING BILL

The all-night session of the House of Representatives and the dramatic passage of the Postal Savings bill had a stimulating effect upon all the members of Congress. There was no longer a disposition to lag, and the policy of marking time was abandoned in favor of the new programme of progress. As a consequence, committee meetings were being held in all parts of the Capitol and bills that had been slumbering for many months were taken from pigeon holes and given the consideration to which they were entitled.

On the third morning after the night session a notice went out that a meeting of the Committee on Naval Affairs would be held at four o'clock that afternoon, for the purpose of taking up the final consideration of the bills that were pending before the Committee.

The notice was like a call to arms to John Carlton. He sent out notices at once to the members of the Committee whom he knew to be friendly, asking them to make it a point to be present for the purpose of helping his bill. Barry happened to come in just about that time, and he utilized the boy in a number of ways.

"I know that you want to be on the field when this battle takes place," he said, laughingly. "I look on you as my mascot, and if we win you will get all the glory."

Barry protested, but Mr. Carlton humorously insisted that he must have his own way in matters of this kind.

There was no doubt about the interest in the Naval Repair Station bill. Copies of the measure had been printed some time before, but the demand for them was so great that the supply had already been exhausted. Several members called during the course of the morning and asked for duplicates of the bill, but Mr. Carlton was unable to accommodate them.

Just about noon time Mr. Benedict, one of his close friends, entered the office and said in a mysterious way:

"John, I hear that your bill is coming up for consideration today?"

"That's correct," was the response, "and I hope you'll be on hand."

"Sure," was the response, "but see here, I heard last night that some change had been made in the phraseology of the Act. If that is so, it will have to go over to be printed and that will cause a delay of at least two weeks in your bill."

"I think you must be mistaken," was the reply. "The bill was in perfect shape

THE MISSING BILL

at the last meeting of the Committee, and I am positive that no amendments of any kind were offered."

"That may be," was the response, "but if I were in your place I'd make sure of it."

Carlton thought that this was good advice, and he summoned Barry to his side.

"My boy," he said, "I want you to go over to the headquarters of the Committee on Naval Affairs. You'll find Mr. Joel Phipps, the Committee clerk, in charge. Tell him I want to see the Committee's copy of the Naval Station bill."

Barry hurried off at once. He found the room without any difficulty. Joel Phipps was there very busily engaged with several Congressmen. Barry had to wait his turn and finally when the clerk was at leisure, explained his mission. Phipps did not take his visit kindly; in fact, he was distinctly disagreeable.

"I am too busy to bother with matters of this kind today," he said.

"Shall I give that message to Mr. Carlton," cried Barry, in a challenging tone.

"No," was the grumbling reply. "Just sit down there and I'll find the bill for you."

He dug down amongst the papers and finally fished out the desired document. He handed it to the boy with very bad grace, and then turned to attend to the wants of several other visitors who had arrived in the meantime. Barry felt very angry at Joel Phipps, but he was forced to admit that the clerk was an extremely busy man, and that probably there was some justification for his irritation. A man that has to attend to a dozen things within as many minutes can scarcely be blamed if he is not blessed with an angelic temperament.

Carlton read the bill over very carefully and found that it was flawless. He handed it back to Barry.

"Leave it with the clerk of the Committee when you go to your lunch," he said. "It's all a false alarm. The bill is all right."

For the next two or three hours Mr. Carlton found his time fully occupied. He had a large mail to answer, and after that he attended a Committee meeting. As soon as he had finished he hastened to attend the regular session of the House. At half-past three he looked at his watch and realized that he would have to leave his seat if he expected to get a bite of lunch before the meeting of the Committee on Naval Affairs. On the way out he was stopped by one or two friends who wanted him to do favors for them.

The clock was striking four when the Congressman entered the room occupied by the Committee; the Chairman had just summoned the members to order, and the clerk was engaged in calling the roll. While these preliminaries were going on John Carlton made a hasty count of noses. He found that there were seventeen members present, and by a careful calculation he felt sure that at least ten of these would vote in favor of the Cleverly bill. To make sure of it, he quietly slipped around from one to the other and confirmed his first estimate. The clerk had finished the roll call, and the Congressman arose in his seat with a great deal of confidence.

"Mr. Chairman," he said, "I move that the Committee now take up for consideration the bill making an appropriation for a Naval Repair Station at Cleverly."

"The members have heard the motion," said the presiding officer, "all in favor will please say aye."

There was a chorus of ayes, and the Chairman declared the motion carried. "The clerk of the Committee," he said, "will now read the bill."

Joel Phipps turned to the pile of papers in front of him and began turning them over one by one. He reached the bottom of the heap without discovering the Cleverly bill. Then he turned them over and went through the pile again, very carefully and very painstakingly. A look of perplexity gathered on his face. The members were becoming impatient. The Chairman seemed to voice the opinion of his colleagues.

"The clerk will read the bill," he said, curtly.

"In a moment, sir," said Phipps, in an agitated voice.

He continued to fumble among the documents on his desk. He looked very much embarrassed. He moistened his lips with his tongue and then looked about the room helplessly.

"Well," demanded John Carlton, "why don't you read the bill?"

"I am sorry to say that I can't find it."

"How is that?"

"I don't know, sir; but I can't put my hand on it."

"Well," said Carlton, addressing the Chairman, "I have a typewritten copy of the measure in my pocket, and if the Chairman is agreeable, I will have that read in place of the original bill."

Jesse Hudson was on his feet in an instant.

"I object," he shouted. "I object to this method of doing business. We have very important matters to consider before this Committee and we cannot afford to transact them in an irregular and possibly an illegal manner. The only bills that this Committee has a right to consider are the bills that are in its custody. If you permit the members to substitute other bills at their pleasure, no one can tell where it will lead nor what the consequence may be."

"But," persisted Carlton, "the bill that I am going to hand you is identical with the one that was in the possession of the Committee."

"That may be," was Hudson's smooth retort, "but it is not the identical bill that was before the Committee. I object to its consideration."

His remarks appeared to have made some impression upon the members of the Committee. Indeed, one of the Congressmen, who was known to be friendly to Carlton, arose in his place and said:

"I think there is some merit in what Mr. Hudson says. At any rate it will do no harm to postpone this matter until the public printer can supply the Committee with another copy of the bill."

"Am I to regard that as a motion?" queried the Chairman.

"Yes, sir," was the response.

"The members have heard the motion," said the Chairman, "all in favor of postponing the consideration of the Cleverly bill for the present will say aye."

There was a loud chorus of ayes.

"All those who oppose it, say no."

A few scattered voices called out "no."

"The ayes have it," said the Chairman, "and the motion to postpone is carried."

Carlton was plainly nettled at the turn of affairs. He turned to the clerk angrily and said:

"I think it's the business of the clerk to take care of the papers of the Committee, and I think it is a great mistake to make a member of Congress and his constituents suffer from the negligence of an employé."

Joel Phipps became white in the face. At this unexpected thrust, however, he had the courage to rise behind his desk, and said:

"I am very sorry the bill was lost, but it's not my fault. The members of the Committee unfortunately have gotten into the habit of taking away papers without obtaining the permission of the Chairman or without giving a receipt for the same. Several of them have done this during the past few days, and Mr. Carlton, I regret to say, is one of the chief offenders."

Mr. Carlton gave a half laugh.

"I guess you're right, Joel," he said, "and I will have to plead guilty."

Nevertheless he left the room in a very dissatisfied frame of mind. The measure in which he was so deeply interested had been thrown back for at least two weeks. That was not the worst feature of the case, either. He had enough votes now to pass the bill. He might not have them when the bill came up for consideration again. The thought rankled in his mind and gave him a disagreeable feeling towards his fellow creatures. As he reached the door of the Committee Room a reporter from one of the Cleverly newspapers, who had heard of the disappearance of the bill, stopped the Congressman and asked him what comments he had to make.

"It's a mighty queer piece of business," was Carlton's reply. "That's all I have got to say."

CHAPTER XVIII
RUMORS OF WAR

Washington is a city of rumors, and for some hours after the mysterious disappearance of the Cleverly bill the air was filled with stories of an approaching political war. Some of John Carlton's bitter partisans made the emphatic assertion that Joel Phipps was at the bottom of the whole business and that he had deliberately destroyed the bill in order to prevent its passage by the Committee. The Congressman was the first one to repudiate this charge.

"There is no proof whatever," he said, "that Joel Phipps is in any way responsible for the loss of the bill. I am a believer in fair play, and I want it distinctly understood that I have not in any way impugned the good faith of my colleagues or of any employé of the Committee."

"But you put the blame on the clerk at the meeting of the Committee."

"Yes," he admitted reluctantly, "I did, but it was a case of hasty judgment on my part."

"Then you acquit Phipps?"

"I have neither acquitted or convicted anyone."

"But what do you suppose became of the bill?"

"I'm sure I don't know," was the despairing reply.

In spite of John Carlton's peaceful talk, the friends and enemies of the bill seemed determined to stir strife. Some of them went so far as to say that the disappearance of the bill was a bit of trickery which had been engineered by opponents of the Administration, who took this method of punishing the Congressman for his loyalty to the President. Carlton pooh-poohed this, but in spite of his protests, the story was flashing along newspaper row. The whole thing illustrated the astonishing rapidity with which a mere rumor can grow into an accepted fact. It was like a snowball rolling down a hill. It gathered weight and momentum as it proceeded. By nightfall some of the sensational journalists were building up a story of a political war that was to involve the entire United States.

Barry missed all of this. He had been sent to Georgetown to obtain some law books for a member of Congress, and he was entirely unaware of the fate that had befallen his beloved bill. Mr. Carlton, in a half amused way, wondered how the boy would feel when he learned the news. He was at dinner in the hotel when one of the newspaper correspondents called on him to inquire whether he would make a statement concerning the great political war.

"Certainly," he said.

The young man pulled out his pencil and note book.

"It will be short," warned the Congressman.

"Very well," was the smiling rejoinder, "anything you may say will be of interest."

"Rubbish!" said the statesman.

The newspaper man looked at him curiously.

"Well, I am still waiting," he said.

"But I have given you the statement you desired," said Carlton.

"What was it?"

"Rubbish—that's all."

"Do you really mean to put that out as your answer to the charges and innuendos that are floating about Washington?"

"That is precisely what I mean. I desire to say neither more nor less. Simply state that Congressman Carlton, when questioned on this matter, said 'Rubbish.'"

While Carlton was doing his best to pour oil on the troubled waters, Hudson was, on the other hand, going about sedulously stirring up the angry passions of the legislators. Without making any direct charges, he insinuated that the proposed bill had a significance which it really did not possess. He still felt very sore over the effective manner in which Carlton had blocked the claim which he presented in the House earlier in the session. A big, broad-minded man would have accepted this defeat gracefully, but Hudson was not that type of statesman. He had a grievance and he nursed it, hoping that in the end he would succeed in revenging himself upon the even-tempered Carlton.

Carlton was still at the table, placidly eating his dinner, when Felix Conway burst into the room, his face red and his eyes staring.

"Sit down, Felix," said Carlton, "and have some dinner with me."

"I don't want any dinner. I've had all the dinner I care for."

The Congressman smiled.

"Then have a plate of ice cream. It may cool you off."

"No; nothing will cool me off, and after you hear what I have got to say, you may be a little warm yourself!"

"Well, go ahead and tell me what is on your mind."

"It's just this," cried Conway, explosively. "These fellows are going around the town trying to injure you. They're putting all sorts of false constructions on your failure to get your bill through today."

"Well, that's no more than I expected;—it's a penalty a man has to pay for being in public life."

"But you don't know what they're saying."

"No," agreed the other, placidly, "and I am not very anxious to hear."

"But," said the journalist, "you've got to listen to me."

"I am listening."

Conway fumbled in his pockets and finally pulled out copies of the evening papers. He opened one of them hurriedly and turning to an inside page, began reading some of the gossip that had been printed concerning Carlton and his bill. The writer said that the whole business had been, as he phrased it, "a grandstand play." He said that it was the belief of men who were on the inside of the Committee that the bill had been purposely sidetracked. He added that Carlton was credited with knowing all about it and that in all probability the bill would never be heard of again. As he finished reading, Conway exclaimed:

"What do you think of *that*?"

"Not much," was the even reply.

Felix Conway looked at his friend in hopeless amazement. He wondered if anything would arouse him. Then he opened the second paper and began to read from that. The insinuations of the second writer were worse than the first. He practically charged Carlton with having destroyed the bill himself, because he knew that it would be impossible to pass it at the pending session of Congress. He said that it was apparently better to lose the bill than to go home and admit to the people of Cleverly that he had been unable to pass it.

Conway threw both papers on the table with a gesture of anger.

"Now," he exclaimed, dramatically, "What do you think of *that*?"

Carlton smiled as the young man indignantly asked the question. He spoke very quietly.

"I think even less of that than I did of the first comment."

Conway seemed dazed.

"Why, you're the queerest man I ever met. Of course, you must strike back at these fellows. You don't propose to let these insinuations stand, do you?"

The Congressman leaned over and put his hand on the correspondent's shoulder, and, speaking in a tone that a father might use to his son, said:

"My boy, I don't propose to do a thing."

"Don't propose to do a thing?" echoed the other.

"No, I do not. If a lifetime of honesty and faithful service is not a sufficient answer to these false and malicious reports, then nothing I can say at this time would have any effect with the people of Cleverly."

Conway looked at him with genuine admiration.

"You've got splendid courage, anyhow," he admitted, "and if you won't answer these reports, I suppose there's nothing for me to do but go back and get out my nightly grind."

"No, Felix," said the other, with an air of finality, "there is nothing else that you can do."

"But," insisted Conway, "if you won't talk for publication, I suppose you will act for your own satisfaction. You will go after these fellows, won't you?"

"No," was the response, "I won't!"

"Well, what in the world are you going to do?"

"Do," smiled the other, "I am going to do nothing. I am going to let events take their natural course!"

CHAPTER XIX
SORELY TEMPTED

It was late when Barry Wynn returned from his errand to Georgetown. The mission he had undertaken for the Sergeant-at-Arms took much longer than he anticipated. When he reached his boarding house that evening, Joe Hart and most of the other boarders had finished dinner. Barry was greatly disappointed, for he counted upon news from Joe Hart concerning the action of the Committee on Naval Affairs.

Barry, it will be remembered, had not read the evening papers or he would not have been in ignorance of the rapid-fire course of events during his absence. Indeed, it must be confessed that the matter of the Cleverly bill, of itself, did not cut much figure in the affairs of the national Capitol. It was really only in its relation to other and greater issues, that it had attracted the attention of the bright young men who supply the metropolitan newspapers with information concerning the latest moves on the national checker board.

After dinner Barry found a letter from home awaiting him. He went to his room so that he could read it in uninterrupted silence. It was a long, gossipy communication, and his mother had evidently been at great pains to give him all the news about the people of Cleverly. She was well and happy, and Hiram Blake was proving himself a most devoted brother. In fact, he had gone down into his own pocketbook on more than one occasion in order to supply her not only with the necessities but the comforts of life.

Mrs. Wynn dwelt with much satisfaction on the letters she had received from Barry. She said she had heard about him in many indirect ways. She alluded to the visit of the Cleverly delegation to Washington, and said that the men were all warmly enthusiastic about the young page boy.

Daniel Smithers had called upon her and assured her with the utmost sincerity that her son would eventually become the President of the United States. When she raised her eyebrows, he had modified his prediction by saying that the boy would at least become Governor of his native state. Then, still seeing some signs of skepticism in her eyes, he had feebly expressed the hope that Barry would at least become the Mayor of Cleverly.

And so the letter went on in an impulsive, good-natured way. It sounded like a chat by the fireside; it was all so familiar and so natural. Finally, the fond mother assured Barry that he was the biggest kind of a success, and that the few little faults, which had insisted upon popping out at inopportune moments, should be utilized by him as the means of arriving at perfection. Barry was sensible enough to realize that his mother was a partial judge, but all the same her letter gave him immense satisfaction. He felt a curious glow of contentment in his heart and he thought, as he stood before the glass combing his hair, that he was a pretty good sort of a fellow after all.

At that moment, of all others, his glance happened to fall upon an evening newspaper that had been thrown across the bed. He began to read the headlines in a perfunctory sort of way. The Cleverly bill had been postponed and possibly beaten. He ceased combing his hair and sat down on the side of the bed like a person who had been suddenly stricken with some physical ailment. Presently, he recovered his breath and read the article through. The statements they contained brought the hot blush of indignation to his cheeks. He felt in a vague sort of way that Joel Phipps must be at the bottom of all this trickery.

Mechanically he finished his toilet, thinking in a numbed way of the misfortune that had befallen Mr. Carlton. One thing he regretted, and that was the fact that he had not been there. He was not foolish enough to think it would have made any difference, but he felt somehow or other that it might have softened the blow to his benefactor.

He was preparing to go to the business school where he had made such progress in stenography and typewriting that he was almost ready to graduate. He was a tidy boy, and tonight, as on other occasions, he changed his suit so that he would make a good appearance before his fellow students. He reached for his coat, in the closet, and put it on. As he did so his attention was attracted by some crinkly substance in the inside pocket; it was bulky, too. He put his hand in and drew out the paper. The sight that met his eyes drew forth a groan of despair.

It was the missing bill—the Cleverly Naval Repair Station bill!

The whole miserable business came to him with a certainty and directness that left no room for doubt. He remembered receiving the bill from Mr. Carlton and he recalled, only too vividly, the message of the Congressman. He was to return the bill to Joel Phipps on his way to luncheon. And he had failed to do so. That was the great, big irritating fact that stuck out like a sore finger.

He thought of the consequences of his carelessness, and he actually moaned. To have failed in his duty would have been bad enough under any circumstances, but to involve the fortunes and the reputations of others was almost too dreadful to think about. He picked up the newspaper and read it through again. Every sentence was like a knife to the sensitive boy.

He remembered with a pang of remorse that Joel Phipps had been accused— at least by innuendo—of trickery. He had thought so himself. What an injustice to a man who was probably better in every way than himself! He looked on the very darkest side of the picture. Suppose, as seemed probable, that the people of Cleverly should lose the coveted Naval Station. They could charge their loss to an insignificant page boy. But that, bad as it sounded, was only one phase of the case. The incident might be the means of ending the public career of John Carlton. The thought brought tears to his eyes.

The newspapers had hinted that the disappearance of the bill would prove to be the beginning of a bitter factional warfare. He tried to dismiss the notion as absurd. And yet, greater events have proceeded from smaller causes. He remembered reading how a stupid cow, by kicking over an oil lamp in a stable, had caused the burning of the great city of Chicago.

At this point in his reflections a new and alarming question presented itself to his mind. Now that he had found the missing bill, what should he do with it? The thought made his heart beat violently. To confess that he was responsible for all the trouble seemed too humiliating to contemplate. The story had become public property. He would be drawn into the limelight. What would Mr. Carlton think? What would he say? How would the announcement of the truth be received by his opponents? They would gloat over it beyond a doubt. Already he could see the jeering face of Joel Phipps.

Suddenly an idea flashed in his mind—an idea so unexpected and yet so plausible that it made him throw himself on the bed. It was simple, and yet, at first, it was awful. It entered his mind in the shape of a question. Why should he say anything about finding the bill? Why not destroy it, or if not that, why not slip it back with the other bills without the knowledge of Joel Phipps or the members of the Committee. It would require a little ingenuity, but it could be accomplished.

He lay there on his back on the bed gazing at the ceiling, and revolving the question in his mind. There hardly seemed to be any room for debate. He had just about convinced himself that he should remain silent concerning his discovery when a clear, small voice cried out:

"Would it be square? Would it be honest? Could you look yourself in the face afterward?"

He roused himself and sat up straight in bed. He looked about him. No one was in the room. The voice that he heard was evidently the voice of his inner consciousness.

Immediately another voice, lower and more persuasive, attracted his attention. It was argumentative. What good would it do anyone, said this voice, to humiliate yourself? The harm has been done. It cannot be repaired. You only injure yourself without benefiting Mr. Carlton. Just forget that you found the bill and that will be the end of the whole, ugly business.

"But could you ever forget it?" warned the small, clear voice. "Wouldn't the remembrance of it hang over you like a heavy cloud? Beside that, wouldn't you put yourself in the position of deliberately deceiving the best friend you ever had?"

Barry jumped from the bed with a physical determination which meant that he had arrived at his decision. In his excitement and eagerness, he spoke aloud:

"I'll go to Mr. Carlton and tell him the whole story."

It had been a hard battle. It showed in his face. But the small, clear voice of conscience had won a decisive victory over the low, persuasive one of temptation. Barry was surprised at the great relief he experienced the moment he arrived at his decision. He still felt very sorry, of course, at his sin of omission, and he was wondering how he should phrase his confession. But outside of these details, his mind was no longer troubled. He had a feeling of mental tranquillity that it would be difficult to put into words.

It was hardly nine o'clock, but he resolved to find Mr. Carlton if he had to tramp the entire city of Washington to do so. He hastily finished his dressing and left the house. Mrs. Johnson was standing at the door. She noticed that his face was pale and his manner determined.

"Is there anything I can do for you, Barry?" she asked.

"No, Mrs. Johnson," he replied, lightly.

But down in his heart of hearts there was an unutterable desire to throw himself upon her bosom and tell her his troubles. How he longed at that moment for five minutes with his mother. But it was decreed that he should bear his burden alone.

He went first to John Carlton's hotel, where he was told that the Congressman had gone out an hour before, leaving word that he would not return until late that night. Barry proceeded on his way to the office building of the members of the House of Representatives. He noticed a light in Mr. Carlton's room. He was shaking now with a nervousness that he could not understand. But his purpose to make a clean breast of the mystery was unaltered and unalterable.

He paused for a moment and then knocked on the door. There was no response. The boy, waiting there like a culprit, began to hope that after all his friend might not be in his office. But he screwed up his courage to the sticking point and knocked again. A familiar voice called out:

"Come in."

The page boy opened the door and walked in the room. Mr. Carlton merely raised his eyes and said pleasantly:

"Hello, Barry; how are you?"

The boy was silent. The Congressman was so absorbed in his work that he did not notice the long pause in the conversation. When he looked up the second time he was startled at the sight that met his gaze. Barry's face was the color of chalk. He appeared to have shrivelled so much that his clothes hung from his body.

"Are you ill?" asked the statesman, with real concern in his voice.

"No," said Barry, huskily; "I've found the bill!"

"Well," laughing and surprised in the same breath, "I'm glad to hear that, but you needn't be so solemn about it."

The boy was tongue-tied. He stood on one foot and then on the other.

"Where was it found?" finally asked the Congressman.

"Where it was not lost," blurted out Barry. "I found it in my coat pocket!"

Carlton's face clouded.

"You come here to tell me this?" he said, sternly.

"Yes," nodded Barry, his eyes on the floor. "It's been an awful struggle, but I had to tell you."

John Carlton was silent for a long, long while. His eyes were never removed from the boy's face for a moment. His own jaws were set in an ugly fashion. But presently it dawned upon him that Barry was very worn and haggard. At once he relented. He spoke mildly:

HIS EYES WERE NEVER REMOVED FROM THE BOY'S FACE FOR A MOMENT.

SORELY TEMPTED

"You know all the trouble you have caused?"

"Only too well," exclaimed the boy. "It was utter carelessness on my part. I would not have had it happen for the world! I—"

"You never returned the bill," interrupted Carlton.

"No; I forgot it. I changed my coat. The bill was in the inside pocket. I found it there tonight. I'm ready to pay the penalty. I'll resign my position if—"

"Barry—" began the Congressman.

"Yes, sir; yes, sir," cried the young page in his agitation, breaking into the other's remarks.

"Barry," resumed Carlton, in a voice that was singularly gentle, "you've already paid the penalty."

"Already paid it?"

"Yes—you've suffered, and you've done the manly thing by coming right to me and telling the truth."

Barry looked at him with gratitude beaming from his eyes.

"You think so?"

"I know it. We all have to pay for our sins of omission and our sins of commission. You've done the only thing that mortal can do. You're sorry; you've confessed—and, I'm sure it will be the lesson of a lifetime."

"I'm positive of that," was the fervent response.

"Well," said Carlton, rising and putting his arm about the boy's shoulder, "you can go home now and go to sleep with a good conscience."

CHAPTER XX
HUDSON PLAYS POLITICS

At ten o'clock the next morning Barry Wynn walked into the rooms of the Committee on Public Buildings, and coolly handed Joel Phipps the missing bill.

"Here is a document that belongs to the Committee," he said.

Phipps looked at the bill and gasped.

"What? The Cleverly bill?"

"Yes; Mr. Carlton gave it to me to return to you before the meeting of the Committee. I forgot all about it. I found it in my coat pocket last night and went and told him. He instructed me to hand it to you this morning. I'm sorry it happened."

The clerk seemed too stunned to speak. When he recovered his breath he broke out into a string of adjectives.

"Well, of all the cheeky kids, you're about the worst I ever met," was the peroration.

"I said I was sorry," said Barry, half resentfully.

Joel sneered.

"You don't suppose you can get anyone to believe that, do you?"

"What do you mean?"

"I mean that it looks like a bit of tricky business on the part of Mr. Carlton and yourself."

Barry's eyes blazed.

"Don't you dare to reflect on Mr. Carlton," he cried. "He didn't know a thing about it. Besides, he defended you before the Committee. Have you forgotten that?"

Joel was mollified.

"That's so. I take back what I said about him. But it looks bad for you."

The return of the bill caused a mild sensation in Congressional circles. Most of Mr. Carlton's associates accepted the explanation by the young page. But a number of others, who desired to make political capital out of the incident, magnified its importance and tried to make it appear that the Congressman had been guilty of the folly of stealing his own bill.

When Barry heard this he was very much perturbed. He hurried to the office of his benefactor.

"I can't tell you how badly I feel, Mr. Carlton," he said; "isn't there anything I can do to make reparation for my folly?"

"No," was the mild reply, "you can do nothing more than you have done. It will be a nine days' wonder and after that it will be forgotten."

"I'll not forget it very soon," said the boy, soberly.

"No," admitted the Congressman, "and Barry, that's the worst of our faults. They leave marks that are sometimes never entirely eliminated by time. My father tried to illustrate the fact for me when I was a boy. He had a fine piece of walnut that he intended to utilize in making a piece of furniture. It was smoothly planed and polished. One rainy day, with the destructiveness of youth, I hammered it full of nails. I was not a vicious boy, but I knew that I was doing wrong."

"What did he say?" asked Barry eagerly.

"He was very much grieved, but instead of thrashing me, as I expected, he made me pull the nails out one by one. After that he gave me a plane and bade me smooth the board off as best I could. Finally I was told to putty up the holes. After that he asked me if I thought the board was as good as it had been before I disfigured it."

"Of course, it wasn't," commented Barry.

"No, it was not. The marks of the nails were still there. And he used the fact to convey a moral lesson. He told me the same thing happened every time a boy was guilty of a fault or a sin,—he damaged his character to that extent. The inference is plain. While we must do our best to repair the wrongs we do, we cannot forget that the scars still remain."

If Mr. Carlton and Barry imagined that the incident of the missing bill was closed, they were doomed to disappointment. While they were still talking, the door opened and Felix Conway came in, his forehead wrinkled with indignation. The Congressman, who was a self-contained man, could not help smiling.

"What's the matter now?"

"Matter enough," retorted the correspondent, "Hudson's playing peanut politics."

"It's the only kind he knows," was the placid retort.

"But you wouldn't think he'd fight a boy."

"What is it?" asked Carlton, with a trace of impatience. "What's he doing now?"

"He's written a letter to the Sergeant-at-Arms, demanding the dismissal of Barry Wynn on the charge of conduct unbecoming an employé of the Government. In a word, he's after the official scalp of our young friend."

John Carlton sprang from his chair, his honest face red with anger. He brought his big fist down on the desk in front of him with such force that the ink bottles danced in sympathy with his passion.

"Well, he won't get it—and you can tell him that for me."

Conway laughed in spite of himself.

"You're not taking this thing seriously too, are you?"

"So much so that I'll stake my reputation on beating Hudson."

But the journalist held up a restraining hand.

"One moment, please," he said, "this is my business, and I'd like you to keep out of it—for the present, at least."

"I'd like to know why."

"Because I have my own notion of the way in which it should be handled."

"All right, go ahead; but I don't propose to sit still and see him hurt the boy."

Barry intervened at this stage of the conversation.

"Mr. Carlton," he said, very earnestly, "I'm very grateful for your good will and your friendship, but I hope you will not permit me to stand in your way politically. I'm not blind. I know that I've brought this thing on myself, and I'm willing to take the consequences. It's not fair to ask you to bear the brunt of my faults, and I don't expect it."

"My dear Barry," said the Congressman, soothingly, "Jesse Hudson's not after you; he's after me. Now, I must either fight him or turn tail and run. Surely you wouldn't ask me—"

"No, no," said the boy, eagerly, "I never thought of that side of it."

"By the way, Conway," remarked Carlton, turning to the correspondent, "did Hudson write privately to the Sergeant-at-Arms?"

The journalist laughed.

"Not much. He gave his letter to all the newspapers. That's what made me hot. He's courting publicity, and I'll bet he gets all he wants before he is through."

"Well," said the Congressman, "what is your desire with me? I know you didn't come here just for the pleasure of denouncing Hudson."

"I want a short, snappy interview with you defending Barry from the charge of intentional wrong. Then I want a few sharp comments on what you think of a Congressman who will strike at a boy in order to revenge himself on a political opponent."

"You know how I feel."

"Yes."

"Well, make me say anything you want. Go as far as you like."

Felix Conway was not the man to do things by halves. He took John Carlton at his word and evolved an interview that was a mixture of brimstone and vitriol. It made the oldest members of the House sit up and gasp with wonder. The resourceful journalist did not stop at this. He had interviews with half a dozen Congressmen, all denouncing Hudson for his cowardice. Finally, there was a cartoon on the front page of his paper. It depicted Hudson as a giant lifting a big club marked "Revenge" against a very small page boy.

Conway made it his business to see that a copy of his paper was placed on the desk of every member. When Carlton entered the House he was surrounded by a group of members who shook hands with him, heartily congratulating him on the forceful interview they had read in the morning paper.

"It was right to the point," said one enthusiastic Westerner, "it was what we call 'hot stuff.'"

Carlton smiled at the recollection of his talk with Conway.

"I only deserve part of the praise," he said; "most of it belongs to our friend Felix. He's the brightest reporter in Washington."

Hudson, on his entrance, found that he was looked upon with coldness. He realized before long that his latest move against Carlton had been a mistake. He was furious over the counter attack which had been made against him by Felix Conway, but he was helpless to resist it. Moreover, such members as did not openly condemn his own charge against Barry Wynn, slyly ridiculed him. He could not stand that. Few public men can stand up against ridicule. So, at the first opportunity, Hudson slipped out of the House and disappeared from view.

During a lull in the proceedings Mr. Carlton left his desk and started for the office of the Sergeant-at-Arms. He met Conway in the corridor.

"Hello, where are you bound for?" asked the journalist.

"To thrash out this threat of Hudson's," was the response. "I'm going to get a copy of the charges, and then it will be a fight to the finish."

"I reckon you won't have much trouble," said Conway, with the Southern drawl that he used occasionally.

"Won't you go along to see fair play?" laughed the Congressman.

"No," was the reply, with a curious laugh. "I've got all sorts of confidence in your ability to take care of yourself, and I have no sympathy with the other fellow."

Five minutes later Carlton was facing the Sergeant-at-Arms of the House. That official, who knew him well, greeted him most hospitably.

"McDonald," said the Congressman, "I understand that charges were filed with you against Barry Wynn. Is that correct?"

"Yes, sir; it is."

"Well, sir, I'm here to answer in his behalf. I'd like to have a copy of the charges. I'm ready to answer them."

"Very sorry," said the other, with a strange smile, "but I can't oblige you."

"Why not," asked Carlton, bristling up at once.

"Because there are no charges now."

"No charges now? What do you mean?"

The Sergeant-at-Arms did an amazing thing. He winked at the Congressman. After that he spoke with a significant emphasis.

"Hudson beat you by about ten minutes; he's withdrawn the charges, and says I'm to consider them as never having been made."

Carlton looked at him blankly.

"Well, that beats the old Harry," he said, finally; "how do you account for it."

"I should say," said the other, slowly, "that Hudson's action was prompted by the force of public opinion."

"The force of public opinion?" echoed the Congressman.

"Yes," repeated McDonald, slyly, "the force of public opinion as represented by Mr. Felix Conway."

CHAPTER XXI
CONWAY MAKES A HIT

In less than a week the incident of the missing bill was relegated to the lumber room of forgotten events. As Mr. Carlton had predicted, other and more important things arose to occupy the minds of the national legislators.

But Barry Wynn did not forget the disastrous affair quite so readily. It remained in his mind as a warning for the future. It was a red light waving him away from the edge of many a dangerous precipice. But blessings often come in disguise, and eventually this lapse proved to be a good thing for the young page boy. He became more careful, accurate and painstaking. He never again postponed until "after a while" the task that could be done at once.

But in the meantime, the incident itself, while forgotten by Congressmen, led to unexpected complications. What had been a single-handed battle between Hudson and Carlton now broadened out until it became a spirited contest between those who favored the reform bills of the Administration and those who opposed them. Like most contentions of this kind, what had been a trivial matter grew to great proportions. The incident of the missing bill might have been likened to a pebble thrown into a placid stream, creating circle after circle until all of the waters were in commotion.

For the next few weeks there was a ferment of factional politics. Even those who tried to keep out of the unpleasant muss were drawn into it as the peaceful waters are sometimes sucked into a fierce eddy. Meetings, large and small, were being held every day. There were conferences, caucuses, and secret gatherings of all kinds. One morning Felix Conway sent for Barry Wynn in a great hurry.

"Barry," he said, when the boy appeared, "there is to be a very important meeting this afternoon, composed of the men who are fighting the reform measures of the Administration. I want to get a good report of that gathering, but I am afraid that if I go to the meeting the members who know me will shut up like clams and I will have my labor for my pains."

"Well," questioned Barry, "how can I help you?"

"Very easily," was the quick reply. "Your shorthand is good, isn't it?"

"Yes, it is. I think I have accuracy and speed."

"Well, you're just the boy I want. First of all, I want a list of those who are present, and after that I would like very much to get a verbatim report of the remarks of some of the principal speakers. Will you help me?"

Barry thought for a moment before replying.

"Well," he said, finally, "if you think that I am competent to do the work, I am willing to undertake it."

Conway laughed.

"There is no question at all about your competency. The only point to consider now is your courage."

"My courage?" echoed Barry.

"Yes, your courage. Some pretty hot-headed men expect to attend that meeting. If they thought that you were there to report it, they would not hesitate to take you up by the scruff of the neck and the seat of the trousers and toss you out of a convenient window."

Barry laughed at this description, and then was silent for a moment.

"Well, my boy," cried the journalist, "if you're not game I won't press the proposition."

"I am game enough," retorted Barry, "but I wouldn't want to do anything that wasn't decent."

"What do you mean?"

"I mean that I would not like the notion of any underhand work. I don't take much stock in this business of peeping through keyholes and things of that kind."

Conway's face flushed.

"You don't suppose I would ask you to do anything that I wouldn't do myself, do you?"

"No."

"Well, then there is no more to be said. This is a meeting of public men to consider public business, and the public has a right to know all about it."

"But you don't care to go there yourself?" suggested Barry.

"No. For the reason that I have already told you. The sight of me would frighten those fellows, and the public would thereby be deprived of information which it has a right to."

"I'll go," cried Barry, ending the parley, "and I will promise to do the best I can for you."

The meeting was held in a secluded Committee room on the ground floor of the Capitol. There were thirty or forty men present, and when Barry reached the door of the room it was pretty well filled. Joel Phipps stood at the entrance scanning the members as they came in. Just as Barry arrived someone called Phipps to the other end of the room, and in the interval while the door was unguarded, the boy slipped in and made his way through the crowd to the last row of chairs. A tall, good-natured member, seeing him, cried out:

"What district do you represent, my boy?"

CONWAY MAKES A HIT

Before Barry had time to respond, another member, glancing at him, replied carelessly:

"Oh, that's one of the page boys."

When the meeting was called to order a few minutes later, Barry found himself almost hidden in a corner of the room. The men around him were so large and he was so small and so quiet that he was completely unnoticed. Joel Phipps called the roll and Barry was able to take the names down. After the members had responded to their names there was a general discussion of the various bills that were pending in the House of Representatives. Mention was made of the fact that the Administration was beginning to bring pressure to bear upon certain members in order to enact various reform measures into law.

The sensation of the meeting came when Jesse Hudson arose and made a spirited attack upon the Administration. He did not mince words. He said just what he thought, and some of his thoughts were not very pleasant. He concluded by saying that he was firmly opposed to certain reform measures that were being backed by the Administration, and that he would vote against them and hoped that other members would do the same.

One or two Congressmen followed Hudson, and spoke in a similar vein. Finally, resolutions were adopted pledging all those present to work together. The meeting adjourned after the appointment of three members for the purpose of gaining recruits among those who had not attended the meeting.

Barry, who had been taking down the proceedings in shorthand, managed to slip out of the room unobserved. He took a trolley car and went to his own room in order that he might be able to transcribe his notes without interruption. In two hours his report was in the hands of Felix Conway. They proved to be the groundwork for one of the biggest political articles that had been written for many a long day.

The following morning Conway's newspaper appeared with a great, big, exclusive story which took the Capitol by storm. It told in detail, not only the story of the meeting, but also the plans that had been formulated for the balance of the session of Congress. The rival newspaper men were furious because they realized that Conway had secured what everybody in journalistic circles call "the scoop of the session." The Congressmen who participated in the meeting were angry at this unexpected exposure, but the President and his supporters, who were backing the reform bills, were delighted beyond measure, and before nightfall Conway was complimented by a letter in the handwriting of the Chief Executive of the nation, inviting him to call at the White House.

CHAPTER XXII
PROOF CONCLUSIVE

There was no doubt about the effect of the publication of the story concerning the meeting of the Congressmen. It was a genuine sensation. It was like an unexpected explosion of a bombshell. There was a run to cover. Nearly all of those who had attended the meeting went out of their way to disavow personal responsibility for having called it together. Others, while admitting their presence at the meeting, and conceding their opposition to certain legislation, said they wanted it understood that they did not endorse all of the rash statements made by the speakers at the meeting.

Jesse Hudson found himself the centre of a raging storm. One after another of the men who had attended the meeting came to Hudson and protested against the publicity they had received.

"What do you mean by involving me in an affair of this kind?" said one big fellow from California. "I'd like to know why you selected me to pull your chestnuts out of the fire."

"You didn't object last night," retorted Hudson, hotly.

"No," was the answer, "but at that time I had no idea that the story of this meeting was to be spread broadcast."

"Nor did I," said Hudson, drily.

Before the day was over the protests became so numerous and so insistent that Hudson was driven in a corner, so to speak. He realized that he would have to do something to save himself from the sea of unpopularity in which he threatened to be engulfed. Finally he began, in a mild sort of way, to deny the truthfulness of the report in the newspaper. He thought, vaguely, that at best, it would be simply Conway's word against his own, and in such a contest, he thought he might stand a chance to come out even.

But Felix Conway was not the man to submit to an injustice of any kind. He promptly sought the Congressman and said:

"Mr. Hudson, I understand that you have questioned the accuracy of my report. I challenge you to refute any portion of it!"

Hudson was manifestly annoyed.

"I have no time to bother with you," he said. "I think you have done enough mischief, and I am too busy to be disturbed just now."

PROOF CONCLUSIVE

Conway laughed joyously.

"Well, I'd like it to be understood," he said, "that I am always ready for a disturbance."

"I'll give you all you want some other time," was the snappy rejoinder.

Later in the day Conway learned that while Hudson admitted that there had been a meeting, he denied the accuracy of the reported speech in which he had been placed on record as declaring himself against the President's policies. This was put out in such a plausible manner that it made an impression on more than one member; hence, before the day was over, there was a general feeling among a large number of the members that Conway, while correct in the main, had taken unwarranted liberties in reporting Hudson's speech. Conway first learned of this impression when he met the venerable statesman who was the Chairman of the Committee that had charge of the press galleries of Congress.

Senator Graves was a statesman of the old school. He wore a high silk hat and a long frock coat, and was smoothly shaven and spoke in well modulated sentences. His whole manner and appearance was against the prevailing spirit of speed.

"Conway," he said, solemnly, "I understand that you have been printing some sensational stuff. In other words, to put it plainly, I understand that you have been sending out misleading reports concerning members of Congress."

"Does anyone make the charge?" asked Conway, quickly.

"No," said the Congressman, "but the report is being circulated so persistently that it gives me great annoyance."

"I can't meet rumor," said Conway, "but if you can produce anyone who makes such a charge specifically, I shall be glad to face him."

"My dear boy," was the reply, "I don't want you to think for a moment that I have any fault to find with you. My experience is that you have never abused the privileges, or broken any of the rules which govern the press galleries of the House or Senate. You know as well as I do how carefully we have tried to guard these privileges, and the measures that have been taken to keep unworthy persons from obtaining access to the floors or galleries of Congress."

"I understand it very well, Senator," was the reply, "and for that reason, I am most anxious to clear myself of even a suggestion of having done anything improper."

"Well, there is nothing more to say," was the response, "as there are no charges, there can be no investigation."

"But," persisted the journalist, "I want an investigation."

"What for?"

"For my own satisfaction and for your satisfaction. I will regard it as a great favor if you will go into this matter personally."

"Well, really," began the other, "I—"

"Senator," pleaded Conway, "I want you to do this as a personal favor."

"Very well," said the statesman, relenting, "if you put it that way I don't see how I can refuse you."

"Thank you, very much, and now if you will fix an hour that will suit your convenience tonight, I shall be glad to bring you the evidence that will convince you that I have acted in good faith."

"All right," was the response, "you may meet me at my hotel at eight o'clock."

The statesman had started away when Conway called to him:

"Oh, Senator, one other word."

"What is it," asked Mr. Graves, pausing.

"I'd like you to have an expert stenographer at your room."

"Why, I didn't think you wanted an official investigation."

"I don't."

"Well, then, what do you want a man to take notes for?"

"I don't. I simply want a stenographer who can read the notes of another person."

Mr. Graves looked puzzled.

"Well, have it your own way. I'll be there, and have a stenographer in attendance also."

Promptly at eight o'clock that night Felix Conway reported at the rooms of Senator Graves. Barry Wynn was with him, and carried in his pocket the book he had used in making his shorthand notes of the afternoon meeting.

The Senator waved them all to a seat and then introduced Mr. Conway and Barry to a young man who was present and who proved to be one of the official stenographers of the House of Representatives.

"Senator," said Conway, in the voice of an attorney addressing a jury, "my evidence will be brief and to the point. I have to present Mr. Barry Wynn, who is responsible for the report of the speeches made at the meeting in question."

Barry, thus introduced, stepped forward and handed his note book to the Senator.

"This contains the remarks that I reported at the meeting," he said. "I have enclosed an affidavit which declares that they are the identical shorthand notes taken by me at the meeting."

"What now?" asked the Senator, looking at Mr. Conway.

"I'd like your stenographer to read these notes."

The young man, thus called upon, read from the book in a clear and distinct voice. The transcript that he made from the notes was identical with the report of the speeches that Felix Conway had made in his newspaper.

"That is sufficient," said Senator Graves, and rising, and putting one hand on Conway's shoulder and the other on Barry's, he said:

"There is nothing further to be said in the matter. You boys know your business. You have the proof conclusive that you were in the right. No one can successfully attack Mr. Conway's report."

CHAPTER XXIII
WHAT BARRY OVERHEARD

John Carlton was very much concerned with the current political developments and felt a particular interest in the storm which had been aroused by Jesse Hudson's ill advised meeting. He was discussing the situation with a fellow member of the House when he was joined by Felix Conway, his Celtic face aglow with enthusiasm.

"We've got 'em going, Mr. Carlton!" he exclaimed.

The Congressman nodded soberly.

"Yes, you've got 'em going, all right," he assented.

The journalist was quick to catch the note of doubt in his friend's voice.

"I hope you're not afraid of a battle," he said, somewhat nettled.

Carlton looked at him a moment before replying. Then he spoke rather deliberately.

"No, Felix; I am not afraid of a battle. I am not afraid of war either. I went through one war, as you know, and I've got some scars on me to show for it. But there is one thing you must not forget. There is hardly ever a battle or a war without a list of killed and wounded."

Conway was disposed to be argumentative.

"That's true," he admitted, "but you will have to admit that it's a glorious thing to die in a good cause."

"It's a glorious thing for the survivors," assented the Congressman, "but I don't know how the killed and wounded feel about it."

"Your bill comes up tomorrow, I believe," he said.

"Yes," responded Mr. Carlton, "and that's what I have been thinking about all the time."

"Don't you feel sure about it?"

"I wish I could. It was all right a few weeks ago, but since this factional fight has sprung up, I hardly know where we stand. You know these contests create enmities that are hard to heal. It's another case of the killed and wounded. You fellows may win your fight against Hudson and his crowd, but my poor bill for the erection of a Naval Repair Station in Cleverly may be numbered among the

WHAT BARRY OVERHEARD

killed."

"I never thought of that part of it," said Felix, "and I am mighty sorry to know that your interests have been put in jeopardy. If I had to do it over again I'd probably change my tactics."

Carlton took Felix by both hands. He spoke fervently:

"My dear boy," he said, "I wouldn't have you do any such thing for the world. I haven't a single regret for anything that has been done. I have been simply trying to look the situation in the face. I know I'm up against a hard fight and I don't want to deceive myself,—that's all. I am not repining in the least, and you will discover that I am not afraid of the fight."

Conway's face brightened again.

"Now, you make me feel better," he said, "but, seriously, don't you think you will get away with the trick?"

"Yes, I do. It's going to be mighty close, but I think I'll win."

"When is the meeting?"

"It has been called for three o'clock tomorrow afternoon."

"By George! That's short notice."

"Yes, it is, and that's why I have been giving some serious thought to the proposition. I have counted noses a dozen times today, and I am willing to take my oath that I have got a sure majority of two votes."

"That's good, but it's close."

"Yes, but in a hot race a nose is as good as a mile."

Conway seemed lost in thought for a while. Presently he spoke in a tone of half admiration and half wonder:

"You know, Mr. Carlton," he said, "the more I think of it the more I am surprised at what you have told me."

"What do you mean?"

"I simply mean that in the face of this bitter factional fight it is almost a miracle that an overwhelming majority of the Committee has not declared against your bill."

"Oh, I don't know about that," was the calm rejoinder. "Men can't afford to lose their heads altogether. Besides, there are other members that have bills that they want passed."

"What do you mean by that?" was the quick interrogation.

"I mean that successful legislation is largely a matter of compromise."

Barry, who had been listening, now spoke firmly but with due deference.

"I don't like to hear you talk like that," he said, "it doesn't sound right."

The Congressman laughed.

"I am surprised to hear you talking in such a strain, Barry. I thought that a boy of your experience would know that life is a game of give and take. The men that come to Washington to represent their constituents simply carry out this universal law in a concrete way."

The page boy shook his head laughingly.

"Now, you 're getting too deep for me," he said. "If you go much farther I won't be able to follow you at all."

"Why, it's as plain as the nose on your face," retorted the other. "Nearly all important legislation takes the form of log-rolling. Theorists who have never gotten down to the rough-and-tumble of real life, look at log-rolling as if, it were a political crime. It is nothing of the sort. It is giving up something you don't want for something that you need very badly, and as long as there is no dishonesty in the transaction I can see no harm being done. You have got to reconcile conflicting interests, and if you do so with a good motive I think you are serving your country."

"That sounds very well, Mr. Carlton," said the insistent Barry, "but I don't believe it's the way the founders of the Republic would have talked. I don't think you can make real patriots believe in that sort of thing."

Mr. Carlton did a remarkable thing. He burst out laughing. Barry looked annoyed. His feelings were ruffled.

"My dear Barry," said the Congressman, "your assertion does not really need an answer. You have furnished it yourself."

"In what way?"

"By your reference to the founders of the Republic. You believe, don't you, that Alexander Hamilton and Thomas Jefferson were high-minded men and loved their country?"

"I certainly do."

"Well, then, let me tell you that the vote in Congress by which the city of Washington was decided upon as the capital of the nation was the result of a compromise between these two men."

"I think I've heard something about that, but I never thought there was anything in it."

"There's everything in it," was the prompt retort. "The people of today have no idea of the bitterness that was engendered during the fight to locate the capital of the Republic. Every city in the middle states desired it, and immense sums of money were offered for the privilege of securing the capital city. The Eastern states had openly threatened secession, and their Northern and Southern members were so bitter that they would not meet together for the transaction of public business. Hamilton and Jefferson happened to meet one day and between them they arranged a compromise by which the present city of Washington, in the District of Columbia, was selected as the capital. The compromise was effected by the Northern states agreeing to the capital being placed on the Potomac river on condition that the Southern states should consent that the debt of the creditor states should

WHAT BARRY OVERHEARD

be assumed by the national Government. The whole affair was patched up at a dinner given by Thomas Jefferson."

Conway interposed with a gesture of mock despair.

"Barry surrenders. Anyhow, he didn't know that he was laying himself open for a lecture on the early history of the Government."

The two men separated laughingly, and Conway promised to be on hand if it were possible for him to render any assistance in the final consideration of the Cleverly bill.

Before Barry Wynn left the Capitol that day, Mr. Carlton suggested that it would be a good idea for him to be on hand at the meeting of the Committee on Naval Affairs the following afternoon.

"It is impossible to foretell just what may happen," he said, "and I would like you to be near by in case it is necessary for me to send out any messages."

Barry promised and went home that night with his mind very much absorbed in the question of the bill which was to come up for final consideration on the following day. He met Joe Hart at his boarding house that night, and after dinner the little fellow told him that he had been given a message to deliver to Senator Graves at the Cosmopolis Hotel that evening.

"I'll go with you," said Barry. "I'm through with the shorthand school, and I feel too restless to stay in the house tonight."

So the two boys walked down Pennsylvania Avenue together to the hotel. Joe went to the desk and informed the clerk that he had a message to deliver to Senator Graves.

"I am sorry," said the clerk, "but the Senator is not in now. We expect him back in about half an hour, if you care to wait that long."

Joe realized that there was nothing to do under the circumstances but to wait. He walked around the corridor of the hotel for a while with Barry, but finally the boys became tired and sat down together on a cushioned seat that had been built around one of the great columns in the lobby of the hotel. It was very comfortable and they enjoyed it very much indeed. The Cosmopolis was one of the leading hotels of the capital, and important men were walking in and out all the time. It was quite comfortable in the lobby and after a while the boys ceased talking. Presently Joe, boy-like, went to sleep. Barry was in a half doze himself when he was suddenly aroused by the sound of a familiar voice:

"Carlton's bill is going to be taken up by the Committee at three o'clock tomorrow afternoon."

Barry's eyes opened wide. He was thoroughly awake, but he did not move nor speak. He sat perfectly still. Presently the voice sounded again:

"He thinks he is going to get it through, but we will have to give him a surprise party."

Someone answered this sally, but in such a low voice that the reply could not be understood by the listening page.

There was silence for some time after this and Barry, moving very slowly and cautiously, peered round the corner of the big pillar, and was rewarded by a sight of the men on the other side of the column. One was Jesse Hudson, the other was Joel Phipps, and the third was a man he did not know. Barry quickly dodged back to his former position and listened very quietly in the hope of hearing more of the conversation. It was unsatisfactory. He only got fragments of the talk. Occasionally Hudson raised his voice, but the stranger invariably answered in a whisper. The boy snuggled up closer in the hope of getting some telltale phrase. In a moment he was rewarded to some extent:

"It hinges on Warrington," said Hudson.

"But he's for the bill," whispered the unknown man.

"Yes," muttered Hudson, "but he must stay away."

"I don't think you can get him to do that."

"I think we can."

"I doubt it very much."

"I don't," was the confident rejoinder. "You know that Warrington loves a good dinner?"

In a few moments the three men walked away, leaving the boys alone on the cushioned seat. By this time Senator Graves had arrived at the hotel and Joe Hart was enabled to deliver his message. Barry did not confide the conversation he had overheard to Joe Hart. He wondered what it all meant. He wondered whether he should tell Mr. Carlton about it. After considerable thought he concluded that it was not very important after all and that, in any event, the Congressman was able to take care of himself. But at intervals during the night he kept hearing a familiar voice saying:

"You know that Warrington loves a good dinner!"

CHAPTER XXIV
THE LAST STAND

Barry Wynn awoke the following morning with a confused recollection of what he had heard behind the big column in the Cosmopolis Hotel. But in the clear light of day it did not take him long to determine what he should do. He resolved to tell the story to Mr. Carlton for just what it was worth.

Immediately after breakfast he hastened to the Capitol, but was disappointed to learn that the Congressman would not be in his office until noon. Barry waited until that hour only to find that it would not be possible for Mr. Carlton to see anyone until later in the day. The boy was in a fever of impatience by this time. He hardly knew what to do. He knew that the Committee on Naval Affairs was to meet at three o'clock and he resolved to stand at the door of the Committee room and intercept Mr. Carlton as he went into the meeting. It was a minute after the appointed time when the familiar form of the Congressman came swinging down the corridor in double-quick time.

"Mr. Carlton! Mr. Carlton!" cried the boy.

"Hello, Barry," responded the statesman, but without stopping.

The young page ran after him and caught him by the sleeve.

"There is something I want to tell you—something important," he panted.

The Congressman slackened his pace without stopping.

"Well, what is it? You must speak quickly. I'm in a mighty big hurry."

"I heard—I heard," gasped Barry, trying to talk and keep pace with his friends at the same time, "I heard that Mr. Hudson was going to try and defeat your bill today."

John Carlton laughed.

"I've heard that myself a dozen times. I can't say it's news."

"But they talked it over last night," persisted the boy. "I heard them—while I was at the hotel."

"I don't doubt it," retorted the other, wearily, "and if I stay here talking to you any longer they'll cook my goose sure enough."

"But I have more I must tell you. I'm sure—"

"Not now," interrupted Carlton.

With that he hurried into the room where nearly all of the members of the Committee had assembled. Barry was in despair. He tried to tell his news and failed. In the meantime Joel Phipps, the clerk, was calling the roll to ascertain whether a quorum of the Committee was in attendance. Barry, at his post in the doorway, could see Mr. Carlton flitting about from one member to another.

While he stood there Felix Conway came along and greeted him cordially. The sight of that beaming countenance was to the boy like a grateful rain upon a parched desert. What he had tried to tell the Congressman he could impart to Conway's receptive ears. Felix listened in silence. At the conclusion of the narrative he gave a prolonged whistle.

"Did you tell this to John Carlton?" he demanded.

"I tried to, but I couldn't get him to listen."

"Oh. I suppose he was so busy that he didn't know what you were talking about."

"That's right. I don't think he knew what I meant."

"I wonder how we can reach him?" asked Felix; then almost immediately answering his own question, he said:

"Thank goodness, he's coming out now."

Carlton was slowly making his way to the door. It was evident from his looks and his manner that something was wrong. His forehead was drawn and his eyebrows contracted with a frown. There was a grayish look about the corners of his mouth. It was rare indeed for this self-contained man to show such emotion.

"Well," exclaimed Conway, anticipating him, "how are things going? Have you got your majority of three?"

The Congressman shook his head with a gesture of disgust.

"No—they've got Curwood. I was sure he was with me last night, but he tells me now that he is going to vote against the bill."

"But that still leaves you a majority of one."

Carlton wagged his head again.

"It would if all my supporters were here—but one's away."

"Who is he?"

"Warrington."

Conway slapped Barry on the back.

"That proves your story, my boy."

"What story?" asked Carlton, quickly.

"The story Wynn was trying to tell you when you went into the meeting."

He smiled in a melancholy way.

"I was so distracted that I didn't really know what Barry was trying to say."

THE LAST STAND

Prompted by the journalist, the page boy himself repeated what he had heard in the hotel lobby the night before. As he concluded, Conway exclaimed:

"What do you think of that?"

"I'm fighting a resourceful crowd," admitted Carlton, sorrowfully.

Before he had finished the sentence, Conway had rushed over to a telephone booth and had the receiver at his ear. He was back in a minute, his face flushed.

"I've had Warrington's apartments. His housekeeper tells me that he went to Wynnwood this morning. He told her he would take dinner there and return in time for the meeting of your Committee this afternoon. Barry," he concluded, "get me a suburban timetable."

Quickly the page boy returned with a railroad schedule. Conway looked it over feverishly. He gave a groan.

"What's the matter?" asked Carlton.

"There's only one train out of that one-horse town this afternoon."

"I guess one train is sufficient to carry Warrington," retorted Carlton, with forced gaiety.

"Yes," said the other, dropping the timetable with a gesture of disgust, "but it won't leave Wynnwood until half-past four. That means that he can't get here until after five o'clock."

"What does that mean?" asked the Congressman, anxiously.

"It means that your bill is beaten unless you can have it amended tomorrow."

"That's out of the question," admitted the other, "tomorrow is the last day of the session, and it will be a physical impossibility to have the general bill reopened for changes of any kind."

"Do you believe in Warrington?" asked the journalist.

"As I believe in myself. He's careless, but he's as true as steel. He's gone away in the full belief that he would get back in time. I'd stake my life on his loyalty."

"When will the Committee reach your bill?"

"By four o'clock at the latest. There are only two bills ahead of it."

"How long will it take to dispose of it?"

"I should say it will either be passed or killed by half-past four."

Conway shook his fist at an imaginary foe.

"The rascals! They've timed it perfectly."

"How?"

"Warrington will only be taking the train for Washington at that time."

Conway paced the width of the corridor two or three times. Suddenly he paused, a look of resolution in his eyes.

"Is debate restricted to the Committee?" he asked, unexpectedly.

"No."

"Then, by Jove, I think I have it. It's only a chance in a thousand, but it's worth trying."

During the next few minutes the journalist showed the latent possibilities that reposed beneath his placid exterior. He hustled Barry to his rooms for certain papers. Joe Hart, who happened along, was hurried off on another errand. All the while Conway was talking in quick, jerky, excited whispers to John Carlton. Barry and Joe returned about the same time, loaded down with reports and pamphlets. These were placed in the arms of the astonished Congressman.

"Now, Carlton," was the farewell greeting of the correspondent, "I'm going to take Barry with me. I may need him. Joe Hart will stay here in case you need his services. In the meantime, good-bye and good luck."

He was off like a flash. John Carlton returned to the Committee room and silently took his seat. His quiet demeanor surprised Hudson. He looked for an outbreak of some sort. But, instead the man from Maine sat there as mute as though he had been deprived of the power of speech.

"Takes defeat better than I expected," whispered Hudson to his neighbor.

"Oh," was the confident rejoinder, "he sees he's up against it and knows there's no use in making a fight."

The Committee proceeded with its work mechanically. The two bills that were ahead of the Cleverly measure were taken up in their order. The sponsor of the first one was about to make some remarks in its favor when the Chairman said that as there did not appear to be any opposition to the bill, there was scarcely any need for debate. Carlton was on his feet at once.

"I think the gentleman should have the privilege of saying what he pleases."

No one objected, and the legislator proceeded to orate for the space of fifteen minutes. It was that much time killed. The Committee voted unanimously to incorporate his measure in the naval programme, which would afterwards have to go in the general appropriation bill. The second bill was favorably reported without debate.

The hands of the clock pointed to four when the Committee took up the Cleverly measure. Carlton made a masterly speech in its favor. But the speech consumed a half hour, which many of the Committee considered an insufferably long time. After that Hudson and two of his friends made short, snappy three-minute speeches against the bill. As the last man sat down Hudson called for a vote on the proposition.

But Carlton was on his feet, holding aloft a protesting arm.

"One minute, Mr. Chairman," he cried, "I can't permit the remarks of these gentlemen to go unanswered. It would not be fair to my constituents to do so. I am told that you propose to defeat this bill. Very well. But, before you do so, I demand the right to place myself on record."

THE LAST STAND   121

Cries of "Hear! hear! Go on" and "Give the man a chance," greeted this opening.

The Chairman nodded a reluctant consent, and John Carlton began his speech against time. His desk was piled high with papers, pamphlets, and books. Thus fortified, he gave the members an exhibition of old-fashioned, backwoods oratory. Whenever he was at a loss for a new idea he would reach over, pick up a book and begin to read extracts from some ancient report. He sketched the art of building navies from its beginning down to the present era. He read portions of messages from the great architects of the past and present. Finally, he discussed the character of naval stations which should be erected by the United States Government.

The opposition members were becoming restless. Already three quarters of an hour had been consumed, and they wanted to bring the matter to a conclusion. They knew that they had the votes and they wanted to defeat the bill and have done with it.

"I call time," shouted one of them, "the gentleman is talking in the most trivial manner."

Carlton simulated intense indignation.

"The member is insulting," he shouted.

"I call for a vote," retorted the other.

"That's gag law," declared the member from Cleverly in his most dramatic style, "and I hope that it will never be said that such law was ever invoked by this Committee."

The result of this tirade was an extension of time. He talked until his voice became husky, all the while watching the hands of the clock. They seemed to crawl around at a snail's pace. But time moves on in spite of men and mice. Soon the timepiece pointed to ten minutes of five. Carlton talked on. The hands reached five minutes of five. The statesman continued his rambling discourse. The clock struck five. At that Hudson arose in a rage. He could risk no more delay.

"I insist upon an immediate vote," he shouted.

"And I demand a roll call on the request," retorted Carlton.

Everybody knew that this was a dilatory motion. But the purpose was accomplished. Three or four more minutes were wasted. Then the inevitable came. The final call of the roll on whether Cleverly was to have its Naval Repair Station was ordered.

Carlton sank in his seat exhausted. He had come to the end of his resources. He knew only too well that he was short one vote. Joel Phipps with his sing-song voice did his work expeditiously. Four-fifths of the names had been called and Conway had not come with his promised relief. Carlton gave one last anxious look at the door. No one was in sight. He gave a sigh—the sigh of a defeated man, and waited in a perfunctory way for the conclusion of the roll call.

CHAPTER XXV
A RACE AGAINST TIME

After their talk with John Carlton, Barry and Felix left the meeting room together, and, hurrying down the corridor, emerged on the plaza fronting the Southern side of the Capitol. The boy was all a-quiver with excitement.

"What did you mean by dumping all of those reports on John Carlton?" he asked.

Conway laughed joyously.

"That's food for thought. He must feed it out to the Committee by degrees."

"What good will it do?" asked Barry, skeptically.

"It will postpone the vote on the Cleverly bill."

"But the postponement won't do any good unless Warrington gets here."

"You've hit the nail on the head."

Barry had confidence in the resourcefulness of the journalist. He felt sure that he had conceived some brilliant plan by which Warrington could be instantly and miraculously—if you will—delivered to Carlton. He wondered why Conway did not tell him all about it. His hints had not given him much satisfaction. So he spoke bluntly:

"What are you trying to do?"

The honest blue eyes of Felix twinkled. Perplexity was drowned in merriment. He threw up both hands in a gesture of abandonment.

"Blest if I know!"

Barry was so amazed at this unexpected reply that he stood stock still at the foot of the Capitol steps.

"You don't know!" he interrogated in a reproachful tone.

"No," replied the other, putting his hands in his pockets, and raising himself up and down on his heels, "I don't know."

"And you left Mr. Carlton believing that you would be back with Warrington at your heels."

"It was the only thing to do. You must never say die, my boy. Fight to the last ditch, but never surrender. There is always the possibility that something may turn up. The first and most important factor in this fight was delay. We've secured

A RACE AGAINST TIME 123

that. How long Carlton will hold that crowd is more than I can predict. After that we need an additional vote. The vote is at Wynnwood."

"Yes, I know all about that—but I don't see how this talk is going to help," cried Barry, irritably.

"Nor do I," responded the imperturbable Irishman, "but do you know that sometimes in the mere act of stating a difficulty you discover a way out of it."

The boy laughed in spite of himself.

"There's no way of getting to Wynnwood—no trains, I mean," he said.

"Quite right, and Wynnwood, being obstinate, won't come to us."

"If we could locate a wireless operator, we might flash a message to Warrington," said Barry, banteringly.

"Yes," assented the other, "or if we could pick up a flying machine that wasn't otherwise engaged, it might help some."

The boy gave a gesture of dismay.

"While we're out here fooling, Mr. Carlton is probably talking himself hoarse."

Conway suddenly broke away from Barry and started across the asphalted street.

"I've got it!" he shouted. "I've got it! The very thing!"

"What is it?" cried the boy, running after him.

"Look across the street," responded the correspondent, breathlessly, "do you see that big automobile, and do you see that red-haired youth in the front seat?"

"Yes, but I don't see the connection—yet."

"You will in a second. That's Danny Burns. He was in my class at Georgetown. He's the only son of one of the rubber kings. He has all kinds of wealth; money to burn, and oceans of time to consume it."

Before Barry could reply, Conway was hailing the young man in the automobile:

"Danny! Danny!"

The red-haired one turned around indolently.

"Why, hello, you rascal, what's the matter? Running a foot race, or is the world on fire?"

"Neither, you time-killer. I want you to give me a ride in your machine."

"Well, of all the cheek you—"

"You've invited me fifty times," interrupted Felix.

"Yes, and you've declined forty-nine."

"Hurry up, or I may change my mind."

"Jump in," shouted the young millionaire.

In a thrice Conway and Barry were in the machine. After the newspaper man had presented the boy, the amateur chauffeur turned to Felix:

"Where to?"

"Straight South, and I'll tell you all about it as we go."

As the big touring car whizzed along, the newspaper man told his college chum the story of the Cleverly bill. He explained the plight of John Carlton and told of the mysterious disappearance of Congressman Warrington. The question was whether it would be possible to reach Wynnwood and return to Washington before the meeting of the Committee was concluded.

The love of adventure was strong in Danny Burns' veins, and he listened with eager interest. When Felix finished his story, Danny turned the steering wheel over to Conway while he consulted road maps and made calculations regarding the possibility of landing Warrington in Washington at the time appointed.

"Say, Danny," cried Felix, as he reluctantly took hold of the wheel, "I don't know a blessed thing about this machine. I wish you'd run it yourself."

"Oh, it's only for a few minutes. If a chicken or a rabbit gets in your way, run over it. If it's a cow, turn aside. We don't want to help the trusts by sending beef any higher; besides it might scratch the varnish on the car."

For a man that knew nothing whatever of motoring, Felix did fairly well. Once the machine threatened to run into a barbed wire fence, and again it skidded on a slippery stretch of road, but otherwise he managed it very creditably. He was glad enough when the owner of the car relieved him.

"I figure it out that Wynnwood is nearly twenty miles from Washington. Now if we keep up our speed both ways and do not meet with any mishaps, there is a bare possibility that we may win out—just a bare possibility."

Felix groaned.

"That means we're beaten," he said. "When a confirmed optimist becomes cautious, it makes me believe the jig's up."

"What time must you be back?" asked Burns, ignoring the reference to himself.

"Well, the bill should come up at four o'clock."

"Well, that's what I based my calculation upon. You see, it's after three o'clock now."

Barry, who had been listening to the conversation, now spoke:

"I think, Mr. Burns," he said, "that Mr. Carlton will keep the votes back until some time after four o'clock."

"Good," cried the young man, "every minute saved in that way is a minute gained."

"Sure," responded Conway, recovering his hopeful manner at once, "and if Danny could gain a few minutes more with this old tin can of a motor car, we'd come mighty near winning the race."

Danny's answer was characteristic of that spoiled darling of fortune. He pulled the lever back one or two notches and the machine shot ahead as though it were possessed of a thousand furies, each one urging the other on to greater excesses. The shock threw Conway against the cushions and made him shake his fist at his friend in pretended anger. As for Barry, the sudden rush of the machine fairly took his breath away.

They were out in the open country now on a great waste of level land where speed laws could be ignored with impunity. They soon went so swiftly that intelligible conversation was out of the question. The young page boy was enjoying it to the fullest. There was something exhilarating about it that made him close his eyes and breathe a long-drawn sigh of utter contentment. He was perfectly satisfied to remain quiet and drink in the joys of this wonderful ride.

THE YOUNG PAGE BOY WAS ENJOYING IT TO THE FULLEST

But even the whizzing of the wind was not sufficient to keep the youthful owner of the car from talking. From time to time he shouted in Conway's ear, taunting him with being an old fogy and offering to bet anything from a red apple to a hundred-dollar bill that he could drive the next mile faster than he had driven the last one. Felix, who was in momentary fear that the machine would be wrecked and that they would all lose their lives, permitted the jibe of his friend to go unanswered.

But the longest journeys have their end, and presently the village of Wynnwood hove in sight. Danny Burns said he knew it, because once, while suffering from temporary aberration of the mind, he had gone fishing there. He said the only house in the place was the old fisherman's cottage where unfortunate visitors were regaled with country dinners at New York prices.

So, being well acquainted with the locality, Danny kept his machine in motion until it reached the front door of the Ancient Mariner of the village. It had scarcely stopped before there was a scampering of feet within and Warrington ran out on the porch, very red in the face and too angry almost for coherent speech. The recognition of Conway caused him to emit a shriek of delight.

"Felix," he cried, "you're an angel in disguise!"

"Why?" asked the wise one, with pretended innocence.

"I've got to get back to Washington at once. I promised Carlton I'd vote for his bill. When I accepted an invitation to eat a dinner here today I had no idea that there were no trains back until four o'clock. I've been telephoning everywhere for a conveyance, but all in vain."

"It's all right," said Conway, quietly, "we came here to take you back to Washington—that is, if you want to go."

"Want to go," he retorted, angrily, "don't you dare to insinuate—"

"I insinuate nothing," was the quiet rejoinder, "but Barry Wynn heard some things last night that convinced me that you would be unable to reach the meeting today unless we came here with a motor car."

Something about Conway's manner rather than his words, caught the Congressman.

"It was a scheme on the part of Hudson's crowd then, wasn't it? I've tried hard not to think so. Conway, I thank you and the boy and your friend. Please put on steam. I want to save that bill if I can. If I fail, I give you my word that I'll make all Washington howl!"

In ten minutes they had started on their return journey. Burns drove his car at a rate that was simply scandalous. The machine ate up the road. It consumed mile after mile like a glutton whose appetite grows with what it feeds upon. Astonished farmers stood at their gate posts and gazed after the queer quartette and wondered if they were escaped lunatics. And Danny Burns, whose recklessness had passed into a proverb, sat there cherubic with delight. Conway looked at his watch. He smiled his satisfaction. He leaned over to his friend and shouted in his ear:

A RACE AGAINST TIME

"Keep it up! You're doing fine! You made the last mile in less than a minute."

At that moment there was a loud report, like the shot of a rifle. There was an unaccountable slowing down of speed and the machine began to limp along like a runner whose breath is exhausted.

"What's the matter?" inquired Barry.

"Nothing," was the philosophical retort, "except that we've burst a tire."

In a few minutes Danny had all of them at work. Warrington, perspiring like a stoker in a fire-room, was jacking up the axle of the machine, while Barry was pulling away on the extra tire which the discreet Burns always carried on the back of his car.

Presently everything was as good as new, but as they started off Felix happened to glance at his watch, and what he discovered made him thump his breastbone in unavailing anger. It was half-past four o'clock, and according to schedule the Committee should be through with the Cleverly bill. He said nothing, because the time for talk had passed.

Presently they came near to the city limits and instead of slowing down, the reckless driver increased his speed. On and on they whizzed until Barry's head ached from the new sensation. They bounced up and down on their seats as though they were rubber balls. A clock in the steeple struck five.

Every one in the car felt that the Cleverly bill was dead and buried by this time. But they kept on with a grim taciturnity that would have been worthy of bigger men in a greater cause. Just as they came within view of the Capitol a young lady, followed by a fluffy little dog, crossed the track of the car. With a trial for homicide staring him in the face, Danny Burns acted with great promptness. He twisted the machine out of its course and undoubtedly saved the life of the girl, not to speak of the dog.

The car skidded up the side of the little park, the centre of which was ornamented with a miniature pond for the cultivation of lilies. The sudden twist of the steering gear gave the machine a terrific jolt. It did more than that. It threw Felix Conway and Congressman Warrington over the dasher and into the midst of the pond lilies. Barry, with the ingenuity of boyhood, clung desperately to his seat in the car.

By very good fortune, neither of the men were injured and they were able to continue their journey. But their personal appearance was a sight to excite the jeers of the frivolous—sopping wet and fantastically decorated with the clinging leaves of the water lilies.

A few minutes later the doors of the Committee room were thrown open and Barry Wynn and Danny Burns hurried into the meeting, closely followed by Felix Conway and Congressman Warrington. The big statesman was coatless. His hair was in disorder, and one end of his collar had been torn from the button. Add to this the fact that the water was dripping from his clothes and that he was fighting mad, and the rest of the scene may be imagined. The clerk, apparently, had just ceased calling the roll.

"Mr. Chairman," shouted Warrington, "I desire to record my vote on the Cleverly Naval Station bill."

There was a tense silence, and then, after a moment's deliberation, the presiding officer said in a hard, cold tone:

"I'm very sorry, but the gentleman is too late. The vote has just been taken and the bill is defeated."

Barry felt as if he would crumple up and fall on the floor in a heap. Danny Burns made his contribution to the general grief in one sentence. He said:

"It's a beastly shame!"

But John Carlton evidently had an inspiration. He was on his feet in an instant.

"I move that the vote by which the Cleverly bill was defeated be reconsidered."

The Chairman looked at him reproachfully.

"The gentleman surely knows that a motion to reconsider can only be made by a person who has voted in the negative."

"Who voted against your bill, John?" cried Warrington, in fine disregard of parliamentary law.

"Curwood, for one."

Warrington lurched over to Curwood. He faced him in a menacing attitude.

"Move to reconsider," he shouted, hoarsely.

Before Curwood realized what he was doing, he had made the motion. The vote to reconsider carried and then the bill was once more placed before the members of the Committee. When Warrington's name was called, his loud "aye" reverberated through the capital. The clerk handed the tally to the Chairman. He put on his glasses and read it to the members:

"The new Naval Repair Station for Cleverly carries by a vote of 10 to 9."

Amid the applause that followed; John Carlton threw his arms around the lily-bespattered form of Warrington and actually hugged him. Barry, on his part, shook hands hysterically with Conway and then with Danny Burns, and all three seemed to enjoy the performance very much.

CHAPTER XXVI
THE HOME COMING

It was the last day of the session, and everyone at the Capitol was laboring under a great strain. The national legislators, with characteristic unwisdom, were trying to crowd the work of three or four weeks into three or four hours.

Several important bills remained to be acted upon. One of these was the General Appropriation bill, which included among its numerous items, a provision to pay for the erection of the Naval Repair Station at Cleverly.

As John Carlton was going into the Capitol with Barry Wynn by his side, Felix Conway greeted the man and the boy:

"How are you feeling after the battle?" he cried.

"Fine," was the genial response of the Congressman.

"Do you think your bill will go through all right this morning?"

"Sure! It becomes a part of what we call the omnibus bill, and as that measure provides for a dozen different objects, I think there will be a general disposition to let it go through without any further change."

Conway shook his head.

"That sounds all right, but if I were you I'd keep my eye on Hudson."

"Oh, Hudson's all right," declared Carlton, "he assured me a little while ago that he would vote for the bill."

Conway looked puzzled.

"Well, that's funny," he said, finally.

"Nothing funny about it. Why, at the session only last night I voted for a bill that he was interested in."

The journalist seemed petrified with astonishment. When he was able to voice his feeling he emitted two startled words:

"You did!"

"Certainly, I did. It was a proper bill and one that should have been passed. I harbor no resentment against Hudson. He is human, that's all; only he was a little more human than most people. He thought I had done him a wrong and he tried to get even with me. I must admit that I do not particularly admire his methods, but I can assure you that I cherish no resentment whatever against him."

Conway whistled—his favorite way of expressing unusual emotion.

"What did Hudson say when you voted with him?"

Carlton laughed.

"He came over and thanked me. He did more than that. He said he was sorry that he had struck below the belt and promised me he would never do it again."

Conway looked at his friend with undisguised admiration.

"Well," he said, "it's no wonder that you are successful. A man who is as charitable as you are doesn't deserve to have any enemies."

The trio laughingly separated, and Carlton hurried into the House, followed by his young friend. He busied himself at his desk for a few minutes and then said:

"Barry, that omnibus bill will go through in a few minutes and after it has been signed by the Speaker of the House and the President of the Senate, I want you to take it in to a gentleman sitting at a desk in that room yonder."

He pointed to a little doorway leading to an apartment finished in marble. Barry was about to ask who the gentleman was when his attention was distracted by a Congressman calling to him.

The greatest commotion prevailed in the House. Everyone seemed to be doing a different thing at the same time. The Speaker pounded his desk; the clerk called the roll; members indulged in short, snappy debates, while the page boys rushed in every direction, tripping over each other's heels and otherwise adding to the general din and confusion. But in spite of the appearance of chaos, the members had settled down to business and were engaged in steadily passing upon bills that yet remained to be considered. Minor legislation, of course, was out of the question. Only three or four of the big bills, like the General Appropriation bill, the Naval programme, the Public Buildings bill, and the Rivers and Harbors bill, were given a place on the calendar.

The House had been in session about an hour when the Speaker summoned Barry Wynn to his side. He had a document before him and had just finished appending his signature to it.

"Barry," he said, in a kindly tone, "take this bill over to the presiding officer of the Senate and have him place his autograph directly below my own."

The page boy did as he was told and returned in a few minutes. The Clerk of the House, who seemed to have eyes in the back of his head, beckoned to him as soon as he reached the desk.

"Go right into that room," he said, "and get the final signature to this piece of legislation."

Barry wonderingly followed instructions. He opened the door leading into the marble room and was greeted by a clerk, who motioned him toward a pleasant looking gentleman, who sat at a big table, signing bills as fast as they were handed to him. He told Barry to take a seat and glanced over the bill hastily. After that he accepted a pen which was handed to him by one of the bystanders and placed his

THE HOME COMING

autograph at the bottom of the bill. It only needed a glance to tell Barry that he was once again in the presence of the President of the United States. He beckoned to Barry. The boy went to his side, and the Chief Magistrate handed him the pen with which he had signed the bill.

"My son," he said, "take this home with you as a souvenir. I understand that you have been very much interested in this legislation, and I think you deserve this little token as a reminder of the success of John Carlton and yourself."

Barry, beaming with delight, hurried to his patron and friend and told him what had taken place. The Congressman smiled indulgently.

"He told me he would do it," he said, in a musing tone, "and I never yet knew him to forget a promise."

Congress sat in session until very late that night, but at the suggestion of Congressman Carlton, Barry made arrangements to return home on the first train the following day. Mrs. Johnson helped him to pack his trunk and he left her homelike boarding house with a feeling of genuine regret. But when he went to the train he did not go alone. He took with him his good friend and confidant, Joe Hart, who, after much urging, had consented to spend a fortnight at the Wynn home in Cleverly. To the delight of the two boys, John Carlton was on the same train and with him was his enthusiastic admirer, Felix Conway.

All four were destined to be treated to a surprise when they reached the little railroad station at Cleverly. The train had scarcely slowed up when the blare of a brass band was heard, and looking out, the embarrassed Congressman discovered that almost the entire population of the city had come to the station to welcome him home and to celebrate his success in winning the new Naval Repair Station for his native place.

Barry's mother was on the platform, in the forefront of the crowd, and he leaped from the train and was soon locked in her arms. In the meantime the procession was forming; an open barouche, drawn by two black horses, had been provided for John Carlton, and Felix Conway, because of his loyalty and devotion to Carlton, was given a seat beside the Congressman. Daniel Smithers, school teacher and philosopher, was chief marshal of the procession, an honor that he carried blushingly and with all due modesty. His assistants were Postmaster Ford and Hiram Blake.

Chief Marshal Smithers, as if by inspiration, insisted that Barry Wynn and Joe Hart, should Occupy the other seat in the carriage with Congressman Carlton and Felix Conway. They climbed in amidst the applause of the crowd, and in a few minutes the procession had started on its way, while the band played in quick succession, "Hail to the Chief," "The Star Spangled Banner," and "There'll be a Hot Time in the Old Town Tonight."

Up one street and down another it proceeded, the enthusiasm growing more intense with each passing minute. Presently they passed the home of Barry Wynn, and at that point the crowd, as if in sympathy with the significance of the occasion, redoubled its cheers and applause. As the barouche, containing the four chief persons in the parade, passed on its way, Barry instinctively turned his head, and the last thing he saw with his tear-dimmed eyes, was the figure of his dear mother standing on the edge of the porch, frantically waving a tiny lace handkerchief.

Lector House believes that a society develops through a two-fold approach of continuous learning and adaptation, which is derived from the study of classic literary works spread across the historic timeline of literature records. Therefore, we aim at reviving, repairing and redeveloping all those inaccessible or damaged but historically as well as culturally important literature across subjects so that the future generations may have an opportunity to study and learn from past works to embark upon a journey of creating a better future.

This book is a result of an effort made by Lector House towards making a contribution to the preservation and repair of original ancient works which might hold historical significance to the approach of continuous learning across subjects.

HAPPY READING & LEARNING!

LECTOR HOUSE LLP
E-MAIL: lectorpublishing@gmail.com

Lightning Source UK Ltd.
Milton Keynes UK
UKHW010647090820
367908UK00002B/402